My
Atlantian

By

ALYSIA S. KNIGHT

Heart Dreams
PRESS

My Atlantian
By Alysia S. Knight
Published by Heart Dreams Press
Copyright © 2019 Alysia S. Knight
Cover design: by Kelli Ann Morgan @
www.inspirecreativeservices.com

ISBN-13:978-1-94000-41-9

Also available from Alysia S. Knight

To those who like to step out of the normal for a bit of adventure, happy reading.

Love,
Alysia S. Knight

Chapter One

"You're tense," Anakale, Jerreon Ander's second in command and best friend, said. "You ought to relax. It's over."

"It's not over." Jerreon didn't look back at Anakale. From his vantage point high on the Council chamber wall, Jerreon surveyed the proceedings going on below. His gaze locked on the solitary figure standing before the Council. Jerreon's hands bit into the railing as he leaned forward, though with the acoustics in the High Council Chamber, he had no problem hearing.

Lysias Ptolemaios stood straight and tall, his head thrown back in a stance that showed supreme confidence. Not at all like one would expect of a man receiving his fate for the most severe crimes against their society that had been handed out in eons.

"It is foolishness. They should have binders on him," Jerreon repeated what he'd said several times since the proceedings began. "They should have let me be down there."

"You might be the Chief Council Guardian, but you were Lysias's main accuser. You discovered his plot and stopped him. Your role in this is over," Anakale said in his ever-present logical tone.

"At least, they should have guardians around him." Jerreon shot him a look, turning his attention back below. Light from the full-walled window filled the room with a golden-radiant glow. It was a glorious sight that usually filled Jerreon with pleasure. He just couldn't find anything pleasurable at the moment.

"Lysias Ptolemaios, this is your final opportunity." Chief Council Hyperian's voice carried through the room. "Do you have anything to say for yourself on your actions of deceit upon our people?"

There was no pause, just Lysias's voice cutting through the air, indignation radiating from his words. "You think you can pass judgment on me? You have grown too weak to rule this Council and our people." A murmur started below, but Lysias ignored it. He stretched out his arms like he was encompassing the room. "You think you have stopped me, but you have not."

Jerreon's insides clenched. He released the railing and headed for the stairs. He only made two steps when he heard Lysias voice raise up again.

"I am meant to be a god."

Jerreon glanced below in time to see Lysias bring his hands together in a loud clap that echoed through the chamber. It barely started to fade when a loud explosion took its place. The massive window behind the Council exploded inward, raining glass shards down on the twenty-four men and women of the Council.

Pain flared in Jerreon's side as the percussion slammed him into the railing. He barely caught hold of it before he tumbled over.

Screams filled the air along with debris.

"What was that?" Anakale cried out from where he'd been knocked to the floor.

"Lysias." Jerreon pulled himself up to look below.

Dust settled, but Lysias was gone.

Jerreon scrambled up, ignoring all the destruction around him as he ran down the stairs. *"I am meant to be a god."* Lysias's words played over in Jerreon's mind, and he knew what the man intended. If he couldn't gain control in their world, he would become a god on another. Lysias had a fascination for Earth. Jerreon knew because it also intrigued him. He often ran into the man in the Hall of Studies.

Reaching the main floor, Jerreon put on more speed. He jumped over a fallen column that crossed his path. Anakale called his name, but he didn't slow. He didn't have time. Bursting out the main entrance, he started across the wide quad.

Jerreon caught a glimpse of a figure wearing a crimson jacket and gray pants slipping into the silver-domed building across the way. Lysias was going for the Astersynidi. Jerreon pressed for more speed, lengthening his long stride. There was only one place Lysias could be headed – the Syndais Chamber – to the space bridge. He was going to earth.

People flooded into the quad hampering Jerreon's progress as they rushed to help those in the Council chamber. Another explosion went off, sending up a chorus of shouts and knocking people to the ground once more. Jerreon stumbled barely keeping his footing. Ahead of him the portal into the Astersynidi collapsed, cutting off his entrance.

Frustration roared through Jerreon. He couldn't let Lysias get to the lower chamber and activate the bridge. The problem was the portal was the only access. The Astersynidi sat directly over the strongest energy point on the planet to help feed power to Syndais, the gateway to other worlds.

People converged on the rubble with him. Jerreon felt energy surge around as people stretched out with mind and body to lift debris out of the way to reach anyone trapped inside the building. Jerreon joined the effort concentrating on one of the large chunks of stone. He tapped into the energy in the world around him and cycled it through his body, feeding his abilities.

The rock pulled free and lifted into the air. Jerreon kept tight focus on it until he had it clear, then he lowered it to the ground and turned back, locking on another. He moved it out of the way to reveal a small opening. Jerreon knelt down to survey the pile of rubble. Rocks and debris tumbled down, but the opening seemed stable enough.

"Jerreon." Anakale reached him just as he started to work his way through.

Jerreon didn't wait. "I'm going after Lysias before he can activate the bridge."

"You do not think—" Anakale broke off obviously realizing the answer for himself.

"I've got to stop him." Jerreon crawled down into the opening, pressing his way through. Rocks dug into his hands. Dust rained down on him. He forced his mind out forming a barrier between him and the rock.

Once, along the clamped and debris filled tunnel, he felt like he was trapped. Forcing himself to remain calm, he expelled all the air in his lungs, then reached out and gripped a chunk of rubble and pulled himself forward. Wiggling free and out to the other side, he crawled to his feet, gulping in air then choking as dust filled his lungs.

"You okay?" Anakale's voice echoed behind him.

"Yes. I made it through."

He looked at an older woman who lay crumbled on the floor only a couple feet from him. Jerreon took time to reach out his mind to her but found no life force. Sadness and anger hit him in crushing waves. Her name was Bion. She was a kind woman, a technician who studied planetary energy fields.

Jerreon forced his attention from her to the transport tubes directly in front of him. He wasn't surprised to find a light flashing to indicate they weren't working. He headed for the stairs, passing more people — some alive, some not. Lysias hadn't cared how many he hurt or killed. They were all insignificant to him. Jerreon started to descend the twelve levels. He had to reach Lysias before he entered the gateway, otherwise he would decimate a whole planet just to feed his ego and need to rule.

Jerreon had made it down seven floors when a tingling sensation stirred across his mind. "No!" the cry escaped him, feeding his urgency.

Lysias was activating the Syndais. Once the space-link was up to power, Lysias could enter the portal and he would be gone.

Jerreon leapt five stairs to the next landing and spun, taking the next several levels in similar fashion.

Reaching the final level, a flash of blue light speared out the round window high in the doorway in front of him. The space-link was almost up to power. It could be opened in just a couple of ticks. He sprinted to the door and swiped his hand over the access panel when it failed to open at his approach. There was no response when he tried to activate it, which should have been impossible. His position as Council Guardian gave him override access to all systems.

Not pausing, Jerreon rushed to the maintenance room just across the hall and grabbed a heavy lift-bar that hung on the wall with an array of other tools. At the door, he put in his access code and rammed the pointed end of the bar into the edge of the opening. He leaned his weight onto the rod, while applying pressure with his mind. For a moment, the door held then with a loud pop and a groan, the door slid open.

Jerreon ducked just in time to avoid the chair that smashed into the edge of the door at his head height as he sprang through the doorway. Jerreon swung the bar up to connect with the chair as Lysias brought it back around for another strike. The percussion jarred the lift bar from his hands as Lysias lost hold of the chair.

Jerreon didn't slow. Arms out wide, he leapt over the chair, tackling Lysias. Both men went down, each locking on the other in a power struggle.

Lysias dug his fingers into Jerreon's neck in an effort to cut off his air. Jerreon thrust his arms up breaking the hold then rammed his fist in Lysias's chin. Lysias fell back against a workstation, but didn't stay down. He rolled to his feet, grabbed an instrument from the table and threw it. Jerreon, who barely made it to his feet, got his arm up in time to take the blow, blocking part of it with a mental shield.

Lysias attacked, hitting Jerreon low, smashing him back against a control panel. Once again Lysias's hands went to Jerreon's neck.

"I should have killed you when you first started getting into my business." Lysias's voice growled with rage as he leaned in to add more pressure. "You thought you could actually stop me. You just showed me my true destiny." He bore down. "Why rule our world when I can be a god on another?" Mad fury burned in his face.

Jerreon rammed one fist into Lysias' side, while swinging his other hand up catching him in the side of the head. Lysias staggered back releasing him. Jerreon swung again catching Lysias in a glancing blow but continued to whip around, bringing his foot up. The kick connected solidly with the man's side.

Lysias hissed out in pain as he spun to counter the move. Jerreon dodged back then came in landing another blow. Lysias had him by a couple years, but they were equally matched in height, build and strength. Mental strength they were even also. They were both top levels.

Jerreon felt a shift in the air around him and turned just in time to block a heavy scanner that sailed across the room directly at his head. He spun back ready to meet Lysias's next attack but the man was across the floor, making a dash for the Syndais, the center of which now looked like a luminescent, pale-blue cone.

Lysias snatched a shoulder-pack from a table as he ran past. Jerreon ran after him, making a leapt to reach Lysias before he reached the portal. Lysias saw him coming and swung the pack out and caught Jerreon in the side of the head. Jerreon went down but managed to grab the pack, yanking Lysias back. The man turned on him, kicking out, catching Jerreon in the shoulder.

Jerreon grunted in pain but didn't release the strap he held in one hand while he grappled trying to grab Lysias's leg with his other.

Lysias kicked again then released the pack, stumbling back. He dove for the portal, snagging an energy-control crystal from the panel by the opening.

Jerreon sprang for him locking one hand over Lysias's hand that held the crystal. He slammed Lysias's hand against the side of the portal repeatedly to force him to release the crystal, while locking his other hand onto Lysias's shirt in an effort to pull him back.

Lysias shoved his free hand up in Jerreon's face, forcing his head up. Groans exploded from both men. Lysias drove his fist into Jerreon's side.

Muscles tensed, Jerreon took the blow as he hauled Lysias away from the opening, gaining the advantage until his foot came down on the discarded pack which slipped out from under him on the highly polished floor. Lysias struck out. His fist caught Jerreon in only a glancing blow, but already off balance, it was enough to tumble him back against the control panel. Jerreon lost his hold.

Lysias twisted away, diving for the portal.

Jerreon made a grab for Lysias but missed. In one last effort, Jerreon reached out with his mind as Lysias stepped into the Syndais. He fixed on the crystal still locked in the man's hand.

Power surged from the crystal, the portal and Lysias. Energy swirled in the air, filling the room. Jerreon tried to draw the crystal to him as Lysias willed it the other way.

A sharp crack split the air. Light flashed as the crystal splintered. Caught by the percussion waves that rippled out,

Jerreon fell back, helpless, to watch as Lysias was pulled into the blue mist and slipped away. Anguish flooded through him. He'd failed. Lysias was gone. His last image of him was of the man reaching for the fragments of the crystal that had split apart.

Jerreon expected the portal to wink closed any second without the crystal to stabilize it, but the pale-blue glowed steadily in front of him. It took him a moment to realize the space-link remained open. Energy surged in the room. Jerreon made it to his feet, stepping closer to the portal. He felt the draw from within.

A slight quiver of movement flashed on the floor, catching his attention. Jerreon snatched up a splintered piece of crystal before it could be pulled into the portal in space. He understood immediately what the shard meant. The small piece that wasn't even half the size of his finger was holding open the link between it and its other parts, and he could use it to track Lysias.

A noise behind him had Jerreon spinning to confront the two men and one woman that rushed into the room.

"Lysias?" Anakale asked.

"He made it through. I failed to stop him." Jerreon looked down at the crystal in his hand. He clenched his jaw.

"You all right?" Anakale took a step forward and laid a hand on his arm.

Jerreon nodded.

"You tried. That's all you could do," his friend soothed.

Jerreon pushed energy into the crystal and let it flow through him, bringing with it a certainty. "No. It's not all I can do."

"What?"

Jerreon raised his gaze to meet his friend. "I'm going after him."

Anakale was already shaking his head. "You cannot."

"What I cannot do is leave him loose on Earth. Think what he could do to their planet, their civilization. We cannot allow that to happen. I cannot." He turned to the two people taking readings at the control panel. "Do not close it down," he ordered firmly.

Gargeli, the head of the Syndais team, looked up in surprised. "We need to. The link is not very stable. It is drawing power from the universe."

"I'm going through." Jerreon stepped toward the portal.

The silver-haired man held up a hand, halting him. "I cannot allow that without authorization. It is forbidden. You know that, and even you cannot supersede it."

Jerreon did know, but he also knew what he had to do. "Can you keep it open?"

Gargeli looked at him, then back to his reading. He nodded. "Not for long. It needs to be shut down. The opening was not executed properly. It could cause power rifts on both planets if we leave it open too long."

Jerreon activated the communication link on his wrist, calling up a direct link to Hyperian, the Chief Council. After a moment of no answer, he tried again, then switched to Esteve, Council Second. "Jerreon Ander to High Council. Need immediate response."

"This is Esteve. Where are you?" the Councilman answered.

"The Syndais chamber. Ptolemaios has gone through. I request authorization to go after him. To stop him," he added at the end, clarifying his intent.

There was a pause. Finally, Esteve's voice came back. "Hyperian was injured. Two of the Council have been killed."

The words hit heavy in Jerreon's heart.

"There are only eighteen of the Council left here," Esteve said. "The others have been taken for healing along with Hyperian."

Jerreon understood what he was saying. It would take all those there to vote in favor for the three-fourths vote needed to give authorization, not that he was going to let it stop him. Still, he would rather have his actions sanctioned, because it was clear what his going after Lysias meant. Stop him, as in end his life. Jerreon also figured Gargeli would try to stop him without authorization, and Jerreon didn't want to harm the man.

"There is still much turmoil here, but I'm calling them together for a vote."

"There is not much time," Jerreon stressed.

"Understood."

Jerreon glanced at Gargeli and the tech working over the monitor, then looked at the portal. It still glowed, but Jerreon thought he saw a slight shift in the color. Urgency built in him.

"You can't be thinking of going," Anakale said from beside him. He too stared at the space-link.

"It has to be done," Jerreon said. His heart pounded in his chest, though he knew what he said was true.

"But to find him? You don't know what you'll be facing. It is a violent world."

"I would say our world is a violent world today." Sarcasm tainted his words.

"This is different. You know what I mean. Maybe you should wait until we can form a team, and they can open another link."

What Anakale was saying was reasonable but it also wouldn't work. The more time Lysias had, the more problems he could cause, and the more difficult it might be to find him. Jerreon looked down at the crystal fragment in his hand, closing his fingers over it. He felt a surge of warmth radiate up his arm, almost like it was confirming his action.

"There is no time to wait." Jerreon slid the piece into his pocket, his focus landing on the pack on the floor. He wondered what Lysias had in it. He reached down and picked it up, placing it on a table.

"What's that?" Anakale followed him.

"Ptolemaios was taking it." Jerreon released the fastening.

"He'd been planning this." Anakale leaned forward with him to see what was in the bag.

Most of the space was taken up by a medical kit. Lysias had thought his move out and was not taking chances with Earth's medical advances. There were a couple scanners that could detect metals and other elements, two energy rods, a filtration mask and bottle for water and two large heavy satchels. Jerreon drew one out opening the top. Reaching in, he took out a hand full of the small gold disks.

"Smart," Anakale said. "But I don't think they use that type of currency anymore."

"True, but as it is gold and ancient, it would still be of value." Jerreon wasn't surprised at the coins, but wondered how Lysias had obtained them.

Lysias had planned well. The gold coins were obviously to tide him over until he could steal what he needed. There was no misconstruing his character.

The monitor on the wall chimed. Jerreon dropped the coins back in the satchels and returned them to the pack as images of Council members filled the screen. Jerreon could see the great hall behind them. From the angle they were at, he couldn't see much damage, but his memory held clear the destruction the explosion had caused.

For greed and power, Lysias Ptolemaios had struck at the heart of their people. Jerreon searched among the faces of the men and women he knew well for the ones that were missing – Bakchos, Eugenius, Philipa and Ana. He wondered which were dead but didn't get to ask as Esteve spoke.

"Gargeli, we are sensing an energy flux. Is the Syndais link stable?"

"It is holding, but I don't know for how long. There are minor time glitches occurring, and they are picking up in frequency," the man said.

"How severe?" Esteve asked.

"Minimal, but for every one I would estimate a day on earth passes."

Jerreon jerked at the revelation.

Esteve's frown was clear to be seen. "Is it safe for someone to pass through?"

"At the moment, yes, but, I do not know for how long."

"Then, if we are to send someone, it has to be now?"

"Affirmative."

"How long can we leave the portal open?" Gais, a Council woman standing next to Esteve, asked.

Gargeli glanced at Jerreon then back to the screen. "I don't think we can. Ptolemaios took a crystal. If we were not locked on a world power vortex, I think the link would have been lost already. I would not dare to try opening it anew until we can find the proper crystal to replace it. Not without a lock point opening on the other side."

"But you are positive it is safe?" Esteve asked.

"Yes."

Jerreon felt the air catch in his lungs as Esteve's focus finally shifted to him.

"You do this and you may not be able to return, though I promise, we will do all we can to retrieve you." Solemnity hung on the man.

"I understand." Jerreon pushed the possibility from his mind, focusing instead on those injured and dead, Hyperian and Bion, a sweet older woman who had never caused harm in her life. He locked on to what Lysias would do to the people of the world he planned to rule.

"This has to be your decision. We will not ask this of you," Esteve said.

"I am fully aware of the ramifications of my decision. Lysias must be stopped. He cannot be allowed to bring about havoc on their planet because we failed to stop him on ours."

Almost in the same motion, the heads of the Council gathered in front of the screen raised and lowered.

Esteve cleared his throat. "As a Council, we sanction your pursuit of the criminal Lysias Ptolemaios with any means necessary to stop him. We commend thee for your efforts. Live well, Jerreon Ander." Esteve broke and swallowed hard. "Thank you for what you do for our people."

Behind Esteve several people reached up and wiped their eyes.

Jerreon nodded, then, unable to stop himself, asked. "Who was lost?"

Esteve's lips tightened. "Bakchos and Philipa. They were directly in front of the blast. It looks as the others will survive."

Again, Jerreon nodded. "I will stop him," he pledged.

Turning from the screen, he faced Gargeli. "You said there have been glitches. How many?"

The man glanced down at the monitors. "Eight," he said.

Eight, and each is a day. That meant Lysias had eight days head start on him. Jerreon headed for the portal, not willing to risk another glitch to lengthen the time.

"If we leave the bridge open —" the man started.

Jerreon cut him off. "You cannot leave it open. Do not even try. Close it behind me. Lysias lost hold of the crystal he was using to draw energy and stabilize the link. It will not stay open for long even if you try. It would risk causing damage to our world."

"The crystal he took," the woman tech, who until now had remained silent, spoke up. "It will draw energy from the earth. It originated from there. You will be able to use it to boost your own energy. It resonates with us. You will also need this." She stepped forward and placed a syringe to his neck. "It contains antibodies to counter diseases on Earth. It also has a translation chip that will help you assimilate languages."

Jerreon slipped his hand in his pocket to finger the crystal. He understood what she was saying as he once again felt the hum of warmth flow through him. "Thank you."

"Jerreon," Anakale called him before he could head for the portal. "There must be another way."

"There isn't. You know it."

"This might come in handy then." Anakale tossed him the pack.

Jerreon caught it and slipped it over his shoulders knowing Anakale was right. "Good-bye, my brother." He stepped through the portal before he had time to ponder his actions. Blue light wrapped around him − pulling him. Jerreon closed his eyes and let it take him.

Chapter Two

Kallie Martin looked over the booth crammed with jewelry but didn't see anything that caught her interest.

"Come on. You've got to get something." Melissa turned, holding out a necklace with a fire opal set in silver.

Kallie admired it, liking its look, but it just didn't seem right. She didn't know why. Normally, it would appeal to her. Kallie held up the little bag that had stained glass stars in it. "I did get something."

"Those are Christmas ornaments."

Kallie shrugged. "I like them."

"You ought to get something for you. This is to be a cheer-up trip. Indulge yourself."

"Actually, since I'm going to be out of a job, I really should save my money," Kallie pointed out as she set the necklace down.

"P...lease." Melissa rolled her eyes. "You can get a new job anytime you want no matter what that jerk says and you know it. I still say you go after him."

Kallie almost laughed at Melissa's indignation, but it was too close to her own feelings. "With what proof? It would be my word against his. He was slick, making sure no one was around. It took me three months to realize he was the one leaving things on my desk and that was only because he admitted it when he asked me out."

"I don't think demanding you go out with him qualifies as asking. And, are you forgetting the things he took from your desk as well as what he was leaving."

"I can't prove it."

"Well, it makes me shudder."

An answering tremor ran down Kallie's spine as the image of her ex-boss passed through her mind. "Luckily, I will never have to see him again."

"You're not going to say you're thankful to him for forcing you out of your comfort zone so you can write full time?" Melissa said, reaching over to pick up another necklace, holding it up to look in the mirror nailed to a side post.

"I like that," Kallie said motioning to the necklace. "And, I definitely would not go so far as to thank him. Trying to make a living as a writer is a risky thing. I'll be okay this year and next is looking good, but you never know."

"I know your books are great, and they're doing everything I said they would." Melissa handed the man the necklace to add to the other two she'd picked, and got down to bargaining for them.

Kallie smiled as she watched Melissa, a long-time, best-selling author. Though Melissa was more than twice her age, they were best friends. They'd met at the first writing conference she'd gone to. Something had sparked between them and Melissa had taken her under her wing. Kallie was afraid she might have given up without her.

It all seemed such a silly dream to be a romance author. After all, what did she know about romance? She'd not even had one that could be considered serious.

What she knew about romance was from dreams, and guys coming to her to talk out their girl problems, not about her ever being a problem herself. Except for her ex-boss, and he was the problem – a very creepy problem.

Kallie had no illusion about herself. She knew she was pretty, with her thick, long, light-blonde hair, blue eyes, fine sculptured features. Her body was trim but still shapely. She was also a hair's width shy of six feet four inches tall. In other words, taller than most guys even without heels.

A lot of people said she should've become a model, but her interest ran more to sports than clothes. Still, if she looked around the market she would find quite a few people staring openly at her, especially in the little ocean-side town of Rosarita Mexico. She stuck out like a sore thumb.

"Now, don't go all quiet on me." Melissa drew her attention. She'd obviously finished her haggling as the merchant was wrapping up the necklaces. "Look at this."

Melissa held up another necklace, this one of interlocked silver links. Kallie hardly glanced at it when something pulled at her senses. She looked around but didn't see anything unusual in the packed market. She recognized several people who had also come from their bus tour, three women haggling with a man over purses, an older white-haired couple and a couple with two teenage girls who were at another jewelry booth.

Energy seemed to flare in her body, making her feel kind of breathless. Kallie felt a pull within her so strongly she followed it two booths down. She looked over the merchandise, seeing most of the same things that had been at the other booths.

"See something you like?" Melissa came up behind her.

"No, I …" Warmth surged through her taking her breath away. Kallie looked around again, not sure what she expected to see.

"You okay?"

"Yeah." Kallie shrugged off the feeling and turned back to Melissa, glancing down at the table. "Hey, those would go great with that one necklace." She pointed to a pair of earrings.

"You're right." Melissa picked them up.

"Something for you pretty ladies?" A man who didn't even come to Kallie's shoulder spoke to Melissa but his focus was totally on Kallie. He gave her a big smile that seemed to hold a lot of interest.

"How much are these?" Melissa asked as she held up the earrings.

He looked at Melissa as if realizing that was where his sale was coming from. "Twenty dollars."

Melissa shook her head and started to place them back on the table.

"Fifteen," he said before she set them down.

Melissa paused then placed them down.

"Ten dollars." The man lowered the price again.

Melissa seemed to think again then nodded. "All right." She picked them up and handed them to the man. "You really should get something."

"I …" Again, Kallie's breath caught and her heart pounded. Her eyes slid over the mass of jewelry, locking on a small, pale-blue quartz crystal wrapped in silver wire, hanging on a silver necklace. A shiver raced down her spine as she reached for it.

Awareness hummed across her senses as she lifted it up. There wasn't much sunlight shining through the canopies that covered the shopping area, but the crystal didn't need it. It seemed to radiate with an internal light.

"How much is it?" Kallie heard the words in her mind, and it took her a second to realize that she'd asked the question.

"It is my newest piece. I finished it just this morning. It is on my best necklace. It seemed a shame to put it on less," the man said. "It matches your eyes. Very beautiful. For you, twenty dollars."

Kallie reached in her purse. Her hands trembled slightly.

"I will wrap it for you," the man said hurriedly.

"Don't bother. I'll wear it." She handed him the money and undoing the clasp, she slipped it around her neck. As it settled against her skin, she felt her pulse leap and a rush of warmth flood through her, followed by a feeling of rightness. After a second the feelings eased, then flared again pulling up her attention to a man standing a couple booths away.

Kallie didn't know how she missed seeing him before. He was incredibly handsome. High, strong cheek bones, sharp nose. Great lips, that weren't too full, just very kissable. She froze in mid-motion of doing up the clasp. *Where had that thought come from.* She'd never thought anything like that before, not even with her favorite movie star.

Two prominent things made him stand out. The first was his height. He had to be nearly seven feet tall. The other was his hair. It appeared more white then blond. *He didn't look that old.*

He stared right at her with pale eyes the color of the aqua water just off the beach. He also wasn't abashed at being caught watching her. When his gaze drifted to the necklace, the lines around his eyes tightened. The color of them seemed to spark, but he tilted his head to her in a nod, as if giving his approval.

The clasp clicked closed.

Kallie brought her hand around in front of her, laying a finger to the crystal. It felt hot to her touch. The heat she felt seemed to be matched by the man's eyes. She tried to swallow, but couldn't quite manage it.

Impossible. The sense of the word more than the word itself floated through her mind.

A tug on her arm ripped her attention back to Melissa. "You should have got it for half what you paid. You're supposed to dicker. It's part of the game. What's the matter with you?" Melissa turned her head to the side as if studying her. "Are you okay? You look kind of flushed."

Kallie finally managed to swallow. She glanced to where the man had been standing. He was gone. "I'm fine, but I think I might walk down to the beach for the horse ride now. You sure you don't want to join me?"

Melissa kicked up one eyebrow. "You're not getting me on a horse and that's final. It's one thing you do on your own."

Kallie smiled. "But think of all those romantic scenes of the horse galloping through the surf with the handsome hero on its back." Her lips twitched.

"I can imagine it just fine without wanting to experience it, and I doubt there's going to be a handsome hero. In fact, I doubt there will be any galloping. It will be a walk on a slow, sway-back nag."

"Then why won't you join me?" Kallie prodded.

"Because I was never meant to be on an animal that is that tall. Have fun." She sounded like she was issuing a challenge and there was no way Kallie could win.

"I will. Will you hold these for me?" She held up her stained-glass stars.

"Sure." Melissa took them and put them in the big tote which was the first thing she'd purchased on arriving.

"I'll meet you at the restaurant." An early dinner was the last thing included with their tour before they got on the bus and headed back to San Diego.

"Okay, I'm going to shop a while longer then go sit on the beach. Maybe I'll see you."

Kallie nodded and walked out on the street to where the tour guide had shown them a path to the beach. She followed the brightly colored tiles that led past the restaurant where they'd eat later, down a couple steps and onto the sand. A salty breeze welcomed her. It felt great.

Just up the beach, what she figured was about an eighth of a mile, she could see a group of horses with people milling around them. She headed for them. A hundred yards carried her past the shops and the restaurant. Kallie let peace overtake her.

For years her life had felt incomplete. The last several months had been especially so. But for a couple days, she'd felt like she was on the verge of something – destiny. It was like when she got a contract on her first book, then the three-book contract that followed. She took a deep breath smiling to herself. *Maybe everything would be all right.*

Ahead of her a man with white hair stepped out from behind a dune. Her first thought was it was the man she'd seen in the market, then he turned to her and she saw his eyes. They were a light color, but a washed-out tan like she'd never seen in eyes. They reminded her of a feral animal.

Kallie pushed back the touch of unease that swept over her. She wondered what the odds were of two men so tall, being in the same area, with hair so close to the same color, though she thought this man's hair was a little more yellowish. Like, possibly a bad bleach job.

Then it hit her. They were probably on some kind of team together. Volleyball from their height and builds. She wondered why the dye jobs, but there were stranger things around. Too bad for this guy though. It looked a lot better on the other man.

He looked her over, his gaze coming to rest on her necklace.

Automatically, she raised her hand to cover it.

"I want the crystal. Bring it to me," he said in a low, demanding voice as he held out his hand toward her. There was an odd accent on the words, and it was obvious that he expected her to obey him.

Kallie stopped. She tightened her fingers around the crystal.

"Bring it to me," he commanded.

She shook her head and stepped back.

"You will obey me." He pointed a finger at her then curved it back toward him. His brow creased.

Kallie's head pounded. She fought the urge to go to him. She wanted to run the other direction, but she couldn't seem to get her legs to move.

The muscles around his eyes and mouth tightened.

There was a ringing in her ears.

He started toward her.

Kallie opened her mouth to scream, but nothing came out.

A muscle in his cheek twitched.

She fought harder to flee, but was frozen in place as he stalked toward her.

"You would defy me?" His words lashed out. Kallie felt them like a whip of pain. She couldn't even groan. The best she could get out was a whimper.

The hand stretched out toward her again, this time opening as if he intended to wrap it around her neck. She could picture his fingers squeezing the life out of her.

Kallie tightened her hold on the crystal. "No," she pleaded. The words came out as a hoarse whisper but the sound got past her lips. Bolstered by it, she managed to force her foot up and back.

He took four steps before she managed the feat.

"You will never defy me again." The man's features, which were actually very beautiful, pulled into a tight, horrid mask of fury.

I don't want to die.

"Lysias." A shout came and another man, who looked almost like a mirror-image of the first, leapt through the air from the grassy knoll above the beach.

Relief washed over Kallie leaving her so weak she sank to the ground. She was saved. Kallie didn't know why, but she knew he would protect her, just like she knew this man would have blue eyes.

He was the man from the market.

He slammed into the first man, Lysias, and they both went down. They rolled in the sand. Hands grappled for holds that would gain them the control in the struggle.

Kallie flinched as Lysias caught the blue-eyed one in the chin. He staggered but came back in, thrusting his fist into the tan-eyed man. They locked on each other. Muscles bulged.

They were so close Kallie picked up other differences. The man from the market's bone structure was much more delineated, stronger. Even taunt in fierceness, his features were classically beautiful.

Kallie jerked at the sound of flesh hitting flesh. There was a groan. Kallie shuddered. Together the men moved, each fighting for leverage. Both had long legs and torsos but the man from the market was slightly taller and leaner, narrower in the hips. Oddly calm now, Kallie thought they both could be models of the perfect man, though some people might say they were a bit too tall.

A prickly sensation ran over Kallie's skin like the stir of ozone in a lightning storm. She glanced up expecting to see dark thunder clouds and lightning filling the air.

A series of odd words pulled her back. The two men stood facing each other, about eight feet apart, the man from the market between her and the other man. He said something back to the other man that Kallie translated as a challenge or the meeting of a challenge. He was putting himself between her and the man more than literally. He would defend her and everyone against the man. Kallie didn't know how she knew it, but she did.

Anger flared on Lysias's face. He drew his hands back wide to his shoulders then brought them forward as if shoving something at the man from the market, who threw his hands up as if to ward off a blow. Sand whipped up.

Pressure surged around her. A boom shook the air. Power hit Kallie knocking her back on the sand.

Kallie opened her eyes staring up at the blue sky. She could feel the sand on her back. The only sound that reached her was that of the surf. She blinked, stunned. The ringing eased in her ears, but nothing made sense. She wondered if she'd fallen and hit her head, or had she fallen asleep and dreamed the men. Now, that made sense. They were too perfect to be real.

She closed her eyes and let her mind float to him. His skin a golden tan and eyes clear blue, with just a touch of green in them. They truly were aqua. Something brushed her cheek and Kallie opened her eyes and fell into aqua depths.

"Are you all right?" The words were melodious with their odd accent.

Kallie smiled, glad the dream was not over yet.

His finger brushed her cheek. "I will not hurt you," he said to her in way of assurance.

"I know," she whispered.

His features softened. "Yes." His acknowledgement rang with pleasure as he brushed her cheek once more.

"He did not hurt you?"

"Who?"

"Ptolemaios." Harshness accented the name. "Lysias."

She remembered the name from when he'd jumped. Suddenly, everything rushed back and the dream slipped into reality but the man didn't change. He stayed just as handsome. She blinked several times and nothing altered, but she noticed a slight bruising on one of his cheeks.

"You're real." Kallie reached up and ran her finger tips along his jawline. His skin was warm and smooth. He jerked at the contact as if she had shocked him. Maybe she had, she felt as if she'd just touched a live wire. Before she could pull her hand away, he pressed his fingers over hers.

"My One." Kallie heard the words clearly in her mind.

Chapter Three

Jerreon's lips twitched at her statement. He understood the feeling. He'd been asking himself if she could be real since he'd first seen her. He'd been looking for his One for so long without ever finding her, it seemed impossible that he'd feel the bond of recognition now.

He'd barely reached the settlement when he saw her step out of the large vehicle with the group. She stood out being the tallest woman and with flowing light-colored hair. After the last several days spent among shorter, dark-haired people, where he stood out like the oddity he was on this foreign world, she'd been a beacon to him, almost a glimpse of home.

But it wasn't just her looks that drew him. It had been a pull to his soul that compelled him to forget his search for the crystal shard and Lysias for a short time. He'd followed the group down the dusty street. He'd lost her for a moment when she'd entered a market area, but her essence led him back to her.

He'd spied her again in time to see her pick up something from a table. His attention so wrapped in her, he didn't even realize what she held until he felt the burst of energy that carried her essence even deeper into him – to his heart.

She was his One, his mate, the other piece of his soul, the one to complete him. The question was how did she end up on Earth and what was he to do about it? His first responsibility was to stop Lysias.

He tore his gaze from her face to the crystal. He wanted to snatch it from her. It put her in danger. Lysias would come after it. The problem was, the crystal had chosen her – called to her. He didn't doubt that. Could it have been because she was his mate, and he carried another portion of the crystal, or had it picked up something in her that it too bonded with?

Lysias would come after her. He would want the power the crystal possessed to boost his own power. He just hadn't expected him so soon. He thought he'd have time to set up something to protect her, then find Lysias before he got anywhere near her. Fury burst within him. He'd been wrong, underestimated Ptolemaios again.

He looked into the eyes of the woman. They were a gentle blue, the color of the crystal that linked the energy of this world to his.

My One. The words echoed again in his mind.

Her eyes went wide as if she'd heard the words, which was impossible, but still he reached his mind out to touch hers. Warmth wrapped around him, so perfect he found himself unable to resist sliding deeper, savoring the connection that blossomed between them until he felt her mentally pull back as if she knew he was there.

Color heightened on her cheeks, bringing a beautiful glow to her.

"Are you all right?" He wanted to brush his hand over her cheeks as he had done earlier, and as she had done to him, but now she was alert, he was afraid of alarming her. He thought of probing to see if she'd been injured or if she was scared by what had happened, but decided it wouldn't be appropriate until she truly became his One. She would have to consciously accept him.

She blinked up at him, her beautiful eyes full of wonder. "Who are you?" she whispered.

Jerreon wasn't sure how to answer. He couldn't just say he was her mate. He was sure that would frighten her. From his few days on Earth, he knew the people weren't drawn to their mates like his people were, and for his people there was only one.

He also couldn't say he was an alien. She would think him not right in the head, and she would not even consider him for a mate. And though he could not do anything about forging their union until Lysias was taken care of, he didn't want to harm his future with her.

"A friend." He went with, figuring it was a safe answer.

She looked slightly startled. He wondered if he had used the wrong word, but that was what his language simulator had brought up. He'd been having trouble dissecting the language because he'd been facing three different languages; his own, the one the locals spoke to him, and one they spoke to each other.

He pressed out a feeling of assurance to her, though she didn't seem at all afraid of him. "Are you all right?" he repeated the question she hadn't answered yet.

She nodded and started to sit up. He caught her hand to help her. Energy passed through them. His heart surged.

A small gasp escaped her.

"Are you certain you are well?" He studied her.

"Yes." She pulled her hand free from his and reached for the crystal, her fingers locking around it. "Who was he?"

Jerreon wasn't sure how to answer, but he couldn't lie to her. One did not lie to their life mate, not that she was his life mate, at least not yet. He went for the simplest answer he could. "He is a criminal."

"What is he doing here? And, why did he want my necklace?"

"He escaped and I am after him. I was sent to stop him. He wanted the crystal from your necklace."

"It's just a piece of quartz." There was hesitancy in her words, as if she was already questioning her statement.

"It is a special piece of quartz. It's naturally tuned to a …" He had to search out his mind for the wording, "frequency that is useful."

She looked … skeptical. The word did not feel right but that was what came to him.

"And he wants it. Why?"

"He can use it to draw energy from the planet to strengthen him."

"Draw energy from the planet? How? How can that strengthen him?" Her lip twitched slightly and he felt amusement come from her.

"His mental abilities."

Her brow arched.

"Lysias is very strong, but he loves power. He wants to be stronger. It will be more important to him now that he knows I'm here hunting him."

Jerreon felt the stirrings brush his mind. She was studying him, and whether she had the ability on her own, or the stone was helping her, she was reaching out to him. He wondered what she would do if he talked to her with his mind. It was a talent he had a high aptitude for, but not one he commonly used. Still, it allowed him to understand people's intentions without even trying to read their thoughts.

Suddenly, she shook her head. A smile brightened her face, making her even more breathtaking. "You're teasing me." She rubbed her hands over her face, running her fingers back through her hair, brushing it away.

The action held him enthralled.

"I've never had anyone do something like that to meet me. I believed it was real for a moment." She stood and brushed off the seat of her pants.

Jerreon could only stand and watch her as she totally dismissed him being serious about her.

"My name's Kallie. I guess after all that trouble I can give you that."

"Beautiful," he translated automatically.

"Thank you. I've always liked my name, but of course my parents chose it."

"No, I meant, in my language it means beautiful."

"Does it really?" She looked at him as if trying to decide if she believed him.

"I will never lie to you," he promised.

"Oh." She caught her breath. Her hand went up to finger the crystal again. "I better ... I was going... I was going to take a horse ride." She stepped back but there was a hesitancy in her that was gratifying.

"May I walk with you?" He should leave her, but he hadn't decided what to do about her or the crystal yet. He would always be able to find her again, when the time was right. Now that he knew her, he would be led to her.

But the crystal was a problem. He couldn't steal it from her. It wouldn't be right. He could ask her for it, and he thought she might actually give it to him, but the crystal had called to her. There was no getting past that any more than the call of her to him. He waited for her answer.

It was a little slow in coming, but after she looked up and down the beach, she nodded. "Sure."

He fell in step with her, keeping space between them for her comfort, though he longed to take her hand.

"So what language is that?"

Jerreon wasn't sure how he should answer. "I'm sure you have never heard of it. It is an old language with a root in many, but very ... obscure."

She shrugged at his answer. "So, you are not from here?"

"No."

"You're on vacation?" She probed.

"Vacation?" It took a second to translate. "No, I am on a duty."

Her eyes sparkled, and he wondered why but liked it. "Are you on vacation?"

"Yes. My friend and I just came down for the day."

"Your friend, the woman in the market?"

"Yes. We'll meet for dinner with the group."

Jerreon got the feeling she was telling him this for a purpose, then he understood, it was to know she wasn't alone. He pushed out a wave of assurance and wondered if it was really that big of a problem, then decided that maybe it was. He had met many dishonest people since he'd arrived. Several had tried to rob him, even do bodily harm. He could appreciate her need for safety.

"She did not come to do this ..." he tried to remember what she called it, "horse ride?"

She laughed. "No. Melissa does not like riding horses. She doesn't really like large animals. They frighten her. She's very much a big city girl. I was surprised she even wanted to come here, but she loves to shop, especially for bargains."

"What about you? Do big animals not frighten you?"

"Horses, no. I grew up in a small town in Idaho. I learned to ride when I was young. Though my family moved, I still got to ride every once in a while when we went to visit my grandparents. They're gone now, so it's been a while since I've been." Her gaze came up to meet his. "Do you like to ride?"

Jerreon looked at the animals on the beach ahead of them. "I have not ridden your horses, but I like animals. It is said I have ... an affinity for them."

They reached the group where several people stood not far from a large four-legged animal. Jerreon studied them finding them to his liking.

"Two to ride?" A man came out to them.

Kallie looked up and Jerreon got the impression she was asking if he wanted to ride.

Before he could answer, the man said. "Twenty dollars, a piece. But I will make it two for thirty."

Jerreon wanted to try riding, especially because he could feel Kallie's excitement. He knew he could nudge the man into letting him ride for free but it wasn't right. The man was trying to make a living. Still, it was hard to meet Kallie's gaze.

"I have none of their currency. I will wait for you here." He dipped his head to her and stepped aside, going to where a large black horse was tethered on its own.

"Careful. He is young and not well trained yet," the man cautioned.

Jerreon looked at the horse meeting its gaze. Strength and spirit filled the animal. Jerreon reached out with his mind and welcomed the beast. The horse dipped its head and stepped up bumping his arm with its nose. Jerreon reached up to pet it. "We are fine," he said over his shoulder.

"Ready to ride?" Kallie said behind him.

Jerreon turned back.

She smiled. "My treat."

"Your treat? You mean you pay for me?"

She shrugged. "It's more fun having someone to ride with."

"I thank you."

The man led a beautiful brown horse with a black tail and mane to Kallie. "You should enjoy her. She is a good horse."

"May I ride him?" Jerreon motioned to the black horse.

The man hesitated. "You are a good rider?"

The horse stuck out his head and bumped his arm again.

"We will be fine," Jerreon said confidently, reaching over to rub the horse's nose.

The man studied him a moment then nodded. Stepping to the horse, he lowered the straps that hung down. "That is as far as the stirrups go, but it should be okay," he said looking up. "You are very tall, but your feet will not drag," he said with a grin, handing the reins over.

Beside him, Kallie laughed. "So, I'm not the only one that gets things like that said to them."

"People make comments about your height?"

"When I was younger, I got the 'hey stretch' and the 'how's the air up there'. It didn't bother me though. I liked volleyball. My height was great for that."

"You are not that tall."

"You're one of the only people that would tell me that. Ready to ride?"

He watched as she put her foot in the loop and swung up on the saddle. He copied the motion. The horse moved nervously, but quieted with urgings from him.

When Kallie gave her horse a slight nudge with her foot, it started to walk. His horse moved with it, tossing its head. Jerreon could feel the animal's excitement. It wanted to run.

"We're supposed to stay on the beach and in sight of the town. There's a sign down there to mark the farthest point." Kallie reached down and stroked her horse's neck.

"Can we go faster?"

She looked at him. "He said it was all right to run them but not hard. But you said you've never ridden. Are you sure?"

"My horse would like to run. I would like to try."

"How about a gallop first and we'll see how you do?" She made a clicking sound and nudged her horse in the side again with her foot. It sprang into a faster pace. His horse immediately leapt to match.

Jerreon heard Kallie laugh, and for the first time since coming to Earth, he relaxed. Pure pleasure washed over him. He liked the feel of the animal under him. He knew of horses. On his world they had pilipi which were similar.

But here by the ocean, with the sun shining down, and Kallie beside him, nothing had ever been better.

When Kallie pulled her horse to a stop, she beamed with pleasure. "I thought you said you'd never ridden a horse before?"

"I have not, but I have ridden something similar. This is a fabulous animal. I like it very much. As it seems, you do. Why do you not ride often if you enjoy it?"

"Mainly, because I don't have a horse. I'd forgotten how much I like it. I got busy with work and other goals."

"What is it you do?"

"I'm an accounts supervisor, or I was. I quit recently." A frown passed over her face.

Jerreon wondered what bothered her.

She brightened again before he could ask. "I also write books."

"Really?" That caught his interest.

She blushed. "I doubt you've read anything I've written. I write romantic suspense."

"I am afraid I do not know what that is."

"I write about falling in love and having adventures." Her lips twitched as if she was holding back a smile. "A handsome hero saving the woman from the bad guy."

He edged his horse in closer to her. "I could do this."

"I think I'm to believe you already did."

The weight descended back to Jerreon. His chest burned as he thought of the dead and injured back on his planet. "Ptolemaios will not stop. You must have caution. He hungers for power."

"You said something like that earlier. What do you think he will do?"

"Ptolemaios is cunning and strong. He will kill and destroy whatever stands in the way of what he wants."

"And what does he want?"

He met her gaze straight on. "To rule this planet."

Chapter Four

Kallie stared back in shock, not as surprised about what he'd said as much as she actually believed him.

She recalled the image of Lysias, his pale eyes, the color of the sand on the beach, burrowing into her. His demanding she do as he said, and the compulsion she had felt to do it. She remembered his anger when she didn't. It too was very real. "So, you followed him here?"

"To this town, no. I had not located him yet."

"Then why are you here?"

"I was following the crystal."

Kallie reached for her necklace. Assurance flooded her heart. "You're planning on taking it from me?"

"At first, I was planning to retrieve it. Now, I think it is better if it stays on you. I think it shields you."

"Shields?

"Lysias could not control you. He is very good at manipulating people but, for some reason, he could not control you. I think it might be partly due to the crystal. It will bother him. I fear he will come after the crystal, but if he were to sense a connection between you and me, he would come to harm you."

"There is no connection between us." As soon as Kallie said the words, she felt they were wrong. She glanced over at him. He was quiet, but his eyes intent as he looked back at her. *My One.* She heard the words in her mind again. They burned through her. Her breathing quickened.

When his eyes dropped to her lips, they tingled as if waiting for his kiss. She swallowed, breaking his gaze to look out over the ocean.

"Do not fear. I will never harm you, nor will I let any harm come to you. I will do all I can to keep you safe, but you must be cautious. You will never know when, but I promise you, he will come. That is assured. He will not give up until he has what he wants."

A trickle of fear ran through her. "Well, I'm not staying around here. After dinner, I am heading back to California."

"You are not staying here then?

"No. Melissa and I have been at a writer's conference. It was a great time but since I don't have a job right now, we booked a condo to stay a little longer. We decided to come here for a day before she had to head back home. She wanted to do some shopping."

"You were not planning on this?"

"Being here? No. There was a presentation at the condo about the trip, and we decided to take it." Kallie thought how when she heard of the trip, she'd felt drawn to come. Still, she hadn't been going to until Melissa said she wanted to."

"You were meant to be here," Jerreon said softly.

She looked at him surprised at the comment. "You make it sound like destiny."

"I believe it was. How else was I to find you?"

Kallie wanted to believe he was teasing her, but the look in his eyes appeared way too serious. "Would you like to run the horses back? It's almost time to return them."

"I would like to spend more time with you."

His words flustered her, making her heart pound again. She wondered what Melissa would say about him. She had a pretty good read on people. "We're to meet for dinner. We can probably arrange for you to join us."

"I would like that if it is permitted. I have had a hard time with food here. I have been surviving on rations from my pack, but they are diminishing. The food here is most different."

"What is the food like where you're from?" She urged her horse into a walk, and again his horse followed.

"We use a lot of …" he paused to think, "vegetables, herbs and grains, mixed with meats and fruits. I guess that does not sound so different, but the taste is."

"Well, everyone cooks different."

"Yes, and live. It is not like I thought here. The world is different from what images I have seen."

"Some people struggle for what they get. Have you traveled much?"

"It is hard to explain. I traveled a great distance to be here, but I have not seen much yet. I … landed to the south and just arrived in this town."

"Coming after the crystal?" She prodded.

"And Lysias."

"How did you know it was here?"

"I have part of it." He reached into a pocket she hadn't noticed in his pants. It made her take a close look at his clothes. The t-shirt he wore was blue, the color of the sky, and clung to his body, not overly tight but enough that it delineated the muscles of his chest and arms. It looked like it was brushed silk. She remembered the feel of it earlier. It was soft over the hard muscle of his arms.

His pants were more unique. They were a heavier material, but again soft and stretched with him. A steel gray color, they reminded her of pants she'd expect on a science fiction movie, normal pants but not.

He also wore a type of low-topped boot that hadn't any heel, not that he needed the extra height. She changed her earlier estimation of his height. He had to be over seven feet. She felt short in comparison to him. It was a new experience, one she liked.

He pulled out a piece of quartz, ripping her attention from his clothes. It was twice the length of hers. The color was identical, but it was the warmth that pulsed within her that testified it was the same. They were not just close, or even from the same place. They were halves of a whole.

"You said 'part' as if at one time they were one piece?" she asked for confirmation.

He waited so long to answer that she thought he wasn't going to, though, he had as much as told her earlier.

"Yes. A long, thin rod, the length of my hand."

"How'd it break?"

His jaw hardened. "Lysias and I fought over it. I tried to stop him from coming here, but I failed." Recrimination rang in his words. Pain etched his features.

Kallie reached over and laid her hand on his. The warmth that came from the crystal was nothing compared with the flash which spread up from his hand. She jerked back her hand with the sheer knowledge that filled her. Jerreon was a man of honor. He would give whatever it took, even his life, to correct what he saw as his failure.

His gaze held hers a second. All softness fell from him leaving only what she felt was determination. He looked away. "We should ride back. We were going to let the horses run." His horse leapt into a full run without any signs from him.

Kallie stared after him, trying to figure out what there was about the man she just wasn't quite getting. Always being 'one of the guys', she felt she had a fairly good understanding of men, but Jerreon was different. He was special, and whatever it was that made him different, she knew it also made him extremely important, and maybe not just to her. A shiver ran through her, but she wasn't sure why.

Following, she watched him race across the sand. He rode hard. A natural in the saddle, but it was as if demons were after him. Had he lied about never riding before? Maybe it was all just a lie. What was she even thinking was going on? He'd followed a piece of rock. Was after a criminal that wanted it for its power. It was beginning to sound a little like science fiction. Where was he supposed to be from – the future?

She slowed her horse. Her breath caught. The idea was foolishness, her mind told her, but something stirred in her. "I'm not going there," she said aloud.

Ahead she saw him reach where the other horses were tethered. He swung down and handed over the reins. In a slow, deliberate motion he looked back at her. She pulled to a stop. His eyes held her even from the distance.

Her hand lifted, but this time instead of going to the necklace, she covered her mouth to keep in a sob. Jerreon turned in the sand and strode away. Kallie wanted to call after him, but didn't know what to say, or what to believe. The remoteness in him kept her silent.

When she reached the other horses, Jerreon was nowhere to be seen. She thanked the horse's owner and assured him she had a good ride. After looking around for Jerreon, she gave up and headed for the restaurant. Mounting the steps, she sensed his presence and turned back to the beach. The sunlight caught his white hair, making him a beacon standing on a sand dune a short-ways off.

He was looking after her, she knew. The urge to go to him hit her strong. There were just so many questions running through her mind. The main one – who was he?

"My One." The words whispered across the sand.

Kallie lifted her arm then lowered it before completing a wave. She turned and went inside.

The place was packed with people from the bus. Still, it was easy to find Melissa sitting with the three older sisters, who were having a women's trip while their husbands went to a ballgame.

"So how was the ride?" Melissa greeted her. "You look a touch windblown."

"It was good." Kallie forced a smile. "Definitely interesting."

"Oh, really?" She looked skeptical. "Did you get some good inspiration riding through the surf?" She brought up the earlier comment.

"You could say that." Kallie looked past the balustrade that opened onto the beach. He wasn't there.

"Is something wrong?" Melissa eyed her closely.

Fortunately, food arrived saving her from having to answer, and the women at the table kept everyone entertained with constant banter. Gradually, Kallie relaxed and started to convince herself everything that happened was just the magic of the day. Her mind brought to life a story for her, full of mystery and adventure. Just what she loved to write about but didn't have in her life.

Dessert arrived just as one of the sisters looked out at the beach. "Mmm." The sound rumbled from her. "Now, why didn't I see that earlier? What's Adonis doing here?" Charlene, the older sister, actually smacked her lips.

Kallie looked out to see the dream image come to life. Jerreon stood on the steps, his eyes, locked on her, the color in them seemed to churn with raging tempests. Reality shifted again in her world.

"My, oh my. You are right about that. That is the stuff fantasies are made of. Do you think that chest feels as fabulous as it looks?" Ruby, the sister whose hair matched her name, asked.

"One way to find out. Won't you join us?" Beth, the younger of the sisters who was in her early sixties, called out.

After a second, Jerreon dipped his head and walked up the stairs, coming directly to their table, to the one empty chair across from Kallie. He slid in it without pause. "Ladies." He dipped his head again. "Greetings. I am Jerreon." His accent made the words linger.

The women started to twitter immediately.

Jerreon. Stunned Kallie realized he'd not said his name to her earlier, but she known it. It didn't make sense. Before she could figure it out, a waitress brought out a plate for him. With just a touch of encouragement from the women, he filled his plate from the dishes on the table.

"Do you live here?" Charlene asked.

"No, I am just here for the day," he repeated what Kallie had said earlier.

"Your accent, is it European or Mediterranean?" Melissa asked.

Kallie leaned in a little to hear his response.

"Not either, though there are possibly some ties there."

"Are you on vacation?" Ruby asked.

"I came because I had a duty. I had to find something."

"Really?" Charlene, who was sitting next to him, laid her hand on his arm and gave a wicked look to her sisters.

Kallie had to fight to keep from laughing. If Jerreon was conscious of their ogling actions, he didn't let it bother him.

"Did you find it?" Charlene asked.

"Yes, but I also found a treasure of greater worth."

All the women leaned into him and oohed.

"And, what was that?" Beth asked.

Kallie's breath caught in her lungs as Jerreon looked across the table at her. His eyes like blue spears penetrating her heart. "The missing part of my soul."

His comment sent the women twittering again.

"And, what are you going to do about it?"

Kallie missed which woman asked the question.

"Guard it. Keep it safe, until I can claim it as mine." His gaze never drifted from her.

The women laughed and gave a couple whistles, but Kallie knew his declaration was completely serious. He'd just stated his intentions to her.

He stared at her a long moment before he lifted something to his mouth. She followed the action, her attention focused on his lips, more enthralled than she'd ever been in her life.

Jerreon shifted his attention from her. The conversation across the table turned lighter as the women chatted with him while he ate.

"What is going on here?" Melissa leaned close and hissed in her ear, breaking her from the trance she'd slipped into.

Kallie looked at her, trying to catch her breath.

"His name is Jerreon."

Melissa's brow kicked up in the expressive way she was so good at.

"We met on the beach. Rode horses together."

"And from a horse ride, you get a declaration of love?" The brow arched higher.

"It wasn't a declaration of love."

"Not specifically, but darn close. And I think he was serious. Please, tell me he's not a creep. It would be a shame for a man that looks like that."

"He's not a creep. He's a man of honor. He's duty bound." The words slipped through her. Across the table, Jerreon's eyes came up to light on her, as if he heard what she'd whispered to Melissa.

"Now I am worried. Since when do you talk like that outside of your books?"

"I … it's just how he is."

"Because he said so?" Melissa laid her hand over hers.

"No. Because that's what I felt when I touched him."

"Touched him? Kallie!" Melissa's voice rose.

"Shh." Kallie leaned closer. "My hand on his arm, while we were riding."

"So, you just met riding?"

She knew Melissa was wondering if she'd gone insane. "Actually, we met when he saved me from being mugged on the beach. It's a long story."

"Long story? You were hardly gone over an hour."

That surprised Kallie. It had felt like a long time.

"Jerreon," Melissa raised her voice and asked across the table. "You never said your last name."

"Ander."

Kallie caught the motion of Melissa's fingers under the edge of the table and knew she was Googling him. Melissa frowned slightly. Kallie wondered if she couldn't get cell service, though she knew she had an international calling plan.

"What is it you do?" Melissa asked.

"Security."

Kallie caught the telltale sign of Jerreon's hand clenching. She wanted to ask what happened besides Lysias's escape and find a way to ease his pain.

"Where are you from?" Melissa continued her probe.

"I am a man without a land." Finality rang in his words.

"You have nothing?" Beth asked, joining back in the conversation.

"My duty." He paused and looked across the table capturing Kallie's gaze again. "And possibly, a destiny."

Again, his comment set the women to giggling. But Kallie found it hard to catch her breath.

"You are too much," Charlene said.

He crinkled his brow as if not understanding. Kallie had the urge to reach across the table and tell him it was all right.

There was a clap of hands and their tour guide walked into the center of the room. "If you are finished," she said, letting them know they were, "it is time to load back on the bus. It is waiting just outside the front door."

Alarm hit Kallie at the thought of leaving Jerreon.

"Have no fear," he said, looking at her. "I will be with you."

Kallie could swear she felt the words instead of heard them, or maybe it was both.

"Good-bye," the sisters chorused as they stood.

Jerreon rose and bowed to them.

Kallie came around the table to him. "Jerreon?" She wasn't sure what she was asking.

"Have no fear," he repeated, reaching out to take her hand. His finger brushed over her knuckle, and his other hand came up to caress a single stroke over her cheek. "I will find you again. First, I must deal with Lysias. It is my duty. If you need me call." He raised her hand to the crystal at her neck and wrapped her fingers around it. "I will hear you." This time she did hear the words in her mind.

His gaze again dropped to her lips, and she wondered if he might kiss her, then she felt Melissa take her elbow and draw her away. By the door Kallie glanced back, but he was gone.

"What is with you? I thought you were going to kiss him, and though that is a world class hunk, it is definitely not you. You are Miss Overcautious."

"I am not." She shrugged knowing it kind of was true. "I've just been waiting for the right guy."

"And that was him?" Melissa asked her straight out.

"I think …. Melissa do you believe in destiny?"

"Well, I believe certain things happen for reasons we don't always see, but are meant to be. So, I guess I do. I'm a strong believer in free-agency too. It's not always free, there are consequences. But, are you asking – as thinking he is your destiny?"

"I don't know. It's just a feeling … a connection to him. I'm drawn to him like I have never been to a man. And it's not just physical."

"Are you sure about that? One thing that man is, is an amazing physical specimen, and with that killer accent of his, it's a pretty potent package."

"I think I'm going to tell Justin you said that."

"Justin knows he's the only man for me. You just be careful. Though I guess we're leaving now. You didn't tell him where you live, did you?"

"No, I didn't even tell him my last name," Kallie answered, but inside she knew it didn't matter, Jerreon would find her.

She glanced around once more before getting on the bus. Again, there was no sight of him. They'd hardly got to their seat toward the back of the bus when the engine started. People chattered excitedly as they stowed their purchases and settled in their seats.

Kallie's hand went to the crystal. She wrapped her fingers around it trying to draw strength. Comfort washed over her. She could feel him on the edges of her mind.

He was watching, and he was worried. He wanted her away from this place – safe.

The guide worked her way down the aisle taking count. "All here," she announced loudly and the bus started to move. Kallie became interested as the large vehicle maneuvering a turn around the fountain. It was an incredibly tight fit through a space with pillars on either side of the entrance to the restaurant's courtyard.

A boom shook the bus, and it jerked to a stop. Gasps went up all around her. For a minute Kallie thought they'd clipped a pillar or something. But when she looked, they were clear. Another blast jarred the back of the bus. Several people screamed.

Kallie twisted around. There by the fountain in the center of the courtyard stood Lysias, his feet wide, his arms down by his side but stretched wide, his palm facing them.

"Come to me." The call came clearly to her mind.

Kallie shook her head.

His fingers flexed. The bus shook again.

"No," Kallie said aloud. Fear made her heart pound.

"You cannot defy me. No one on this planet can."

"You want to bet." She tightened her hold on the crystal. It felt like it was beginning to crackle with energy.

"What are you saying?" Melissa looked at her alarmed, but Kallie kept her focus on Lysias.

A child on the bus started to cry as if he could detect something was wrong.

Lysias lifted a hand. An odd blue glow danced in his palm. He brought his arm back as if to throw it. He started to bring his hand forward. The light in his palm flared out, shooting straight at the bus like a streak of lightning. Another stab of light streaked across the courtyard from somewhere behind the bus that intersected the first. They both disintegrated in a flash that rattled the windows.

The bus engine revved to a whine.

In the courtyard, Lysias stumbled back tripping over the edge of the fountain, falling into the water. The bus lurched forward. Kallie didn't remember standing, but she must have because the motion knocked her off her feet into the side of the bus.

By the time she righted herself, she couldn't see Lysias. The bus edged forward past the pillars then stopped. Out the front window, she saw a flash of silver-white hair, but felt no fear.

The front doors on the bus parted. A second later, Jerreon stepped on, ducking down so as not to hit his head. His gaze found her before he stopped to talk with the driver and tour guide. Only a couple seconds elapsed before he walked back toward her.

"I think it is better that I come," he said, then looked at the teenage boy in the seat across the aisle from her, who had hit on her all the way there that morning. "May I?"

"Sure." The kid slid out of the seat and moved into an open one a couple rows back.

Jerreon dropped into the seat. His head tipped back, closing his eyes. Weariness flowed from him.

"Are you all right?" Kallie reached across the aisle and laid a hand on his arm. He opened his eyes, looked at her and put his hand over hers to hold the contact.

"I have not had much rest the last couple days." He linked his fingers with hers and closed his eyes again.

The bus turned onto the main road and started to pick up speed.

"Kallie?"

She glanced at Melissa and gave a reassuring smile. "It's all right."

"Did something more than I know happen back there?" Melissa looked across to Jerreon.

"I think so. I'm just not quite sure what."

Melissa leaned closer. "Who is he, really?"

Kallie wasn't quite sure how to answer that either, wasn't even sure if she knew. She did know he was a good man and he'd saved her, again. "He's a friend. He's after a criminal."

"Who? That other guy back there that looks like him?" Melissa seemed to accept that.

"Yes."

"Well, he's no normal police officer," Melissa stated and Kallie had to agree.

There was nothing normal about Jerreon. She leaned back and watched him sleep, her hand still stretched across the aisle on his arm, held securely by his hand.

Kallie tried to focus her gaze out the window at the beautiful ocean views broken by scattered stately-looking homes and rubble-constructed dwellings. It wasn't long until it became more congested and the little shacks turned into buildings that were stacked on each other with graffiti covering much of their walls. A horn blared loudly as a car cut in front of them.

The fingers holding hers tightened. Kallie looked over to find Jerreon's eyes wide open. He stared out the window. "What is this place?"

"It's Tijuana. It's a border town. We're not driving through a very good area right now."

"I do not know what to think. It is not what I was expecting." He looked so gloomy.

"We'll be to the border soon. You have your passport, don't you?" She felt a touch of panic.

He squeezed her fingers. "I have all I need."

Chapter Five

What was a passport? Jerreon searched the information link on his wrist for clarification but nothing came up. Whatever it was had disturbed Kallie, and he didn't want that. His language translation chip was functioning excellently, though it was still being integrated to his system, and it had gaps of knowledge which unsettled him. Still, he was glad for it.

The bus slowed to a walking pace.

At the front of the bus, the woman in charge stood. "I will be handing out declaration forms that everyone needs to fill out for anything you purchased." She started down the aisle handing out pieces of paper.

He took it when offered then watched as Kallie got a writing implement from her bag. She drew out two small blue books from a pocket strapped to her waist. She opened one and he saw an image of Melissa. Kallie handed it to her friend, then opened the other that revealed an image of her. The likeness was very good, but she wasn't smiling like normal.

Around him other people pulled out similar books. Jerreon realized a passport was an identification document. They had to carry such things instead of their systems recognizing automatically who a person was as he was used to.

Kallie finished writing on her paper and looked at him. "Would you like to borrow my pen?"

"Yes, thank you. May I see?" He held out his hand for the passport.

She shrugged and handed it to him. He opened it, going through the pages memorizing them, pausing on the page with her image. He took extra time there before turning to the next.

"I don't have very many stamps. I haven't been to many countries before, just to Canada and ones on a cruise."

"Do you wish to travel?" He looked to her.

"I like to see new places."

He would like to show her his home, but it was not meant to be, so maybe they could explore hers. There had been some beautiful places that he had seen images of.

"All right everyone." The tour guide stood again. "We are coming to the border. We will all have to get off the bus and go through the building while the bus is searched. Please take your belongings with you. It looks like it won't be a long wait today, about a half hour if we're lucky. Everyone, please stay together. We will re-board the bus out the other side."

Jerreon stood and let Melissa and Kallie go in front of him. They followed the other people ahead of them, moving in a straight line. He listened until he understood what was going on, then he looked around until he detected someone he thought might be in charge.

"I need to talk to that man over there." He leaned down to speak to Kallie. He knew she watched him as he walked away, but he focused on the man. Reaching into his pocket, he pulled out his piece of the crystal. *I hope this works.* He channeled energy through it. "Could you help me pass through?" He nudged compliancy and helpfulness to the man.

"Certainly, if you will just step over here." He led Jerreon to a desk off to one side. "Your passport please."

Jerreon handed him the declaration paper and brought up the image of Kallie's passport in his mind, but with his likeness on it. He willed the image into the man's mind. The man looked at the paper. Then reached for a stamp, stamped the paper and handed it back to him.

"Have a nice day," the man said, motioning him past.

Jerreon kept up the assurance that all was well directed at the man mind until he was outside the building on the other side. Then he released it and relaxed. His body trembled from the drain, but it had worked. The man had seen what he wanted him to see. He couldn't believe it was possible.

He'd had no trouble detecting emotions and strong intentions off people since he'd arrived, but he would have never even considered trying to manipulate them, not until Lysias had tried it on Kallie. Though Lysias's efforts hadn't worked on her, he'd gotten the feeling that it had worked for Lysias before.

"Everything all right?" Kallie came up from behind, startling him. He was so fatigued for once he hadn't sensed her.

"Yes." He turned. "I'm just tired."

"You said you've only been here a couple days, probably a bit of jet-lag."

"Yes," he agreed, not sure what that was. It was unusual, most of what was said to him was easy to follow, but others; he had no clue of the meanings.

"We're in the U.S. now. Have you ever been here before?"

"No. It looks … cleaner."

She laughed. "There are a lot of amazing things in Mexico, but some rough, struggling areas too. The U. S. has areas like that also, but there is a difference."

"I will place myself in your hands to show me."

"That could be setting yourself up for trouble," Melissa said. "I'm just not sure what."

Jerreon felt the woman's scrutiny. He could respect Melissa's caution. She wanted to protect Kallie, but he wanted her to know he would never hurt Kallie. She was his One. He was incapable of bringing her harm. When the link was formed between them, any pain that came to her would come to him.

On his world, the sharing of pain made them stronger and more united. It was not so with all mates, but he knew it would be with him for her. He could already sense her so strongly and the bond was not even formed. *What did it take on her world to have them united?*

He looked up to find Melissa watching him. He wished he could ease her concerns, but he was too spent to try right then. His body was crashing. The food had helped, as had the short rest on the bus, but he'd expelled a lot of energy and needed a full restorative rest. He could not allow that of himself though until he knew Kallie was somewhere settled and safe.

"The bus is through. We can board now." The tour guide ushered everyone toward the large transport.

Once on board, Jerreon sank into his seat, relieved. He wanted to reach for Kallie but his arms felt like stone. He needed to sleep but willed himself to stay awake as he'd been doing the last three days.

All he had been able to think about was that Lysias had an eight days head-start on the world, and what he could have been doing. At least, Lysias had not gotten the crystal. That was fortunate. Still, Lysias had had more time to familiarize himself.

Since awakening on a barren beach, Jerreon felt more than lost. The only thing he had to hold to was the fragment of crystal that called out to its mate. And, if he could feel it Lysias could.

Maybe he should have taken the shard from Kallie. He had no doubt she would give it to him if he asked, but inside, he knew it was the wrong thing to do. It had called to her as much as it called to him. It had brought them together. He reached into his pocket and felt the warmth of energy flow through him. The techs were right. With it, he did pick up strength from the Earth.

Outside the windows, the world seemed to have changed. Transportation units filled the roadways. Those going the other direction were moving slowly but many going their way sped by. He wanted to ask Kallie about them but he wasn't sure how much he should reveal yet. He didn't want to frighten her.

They drove into a city that was far different from where they'd been. There were tall buildings that gleamed in the late afternoon sun. The transport turned off onto a smaller road that wound around, through the buildings.

They pulled up in front of a beautiful structure. A large portion of people got off. When Kallie showed no sign of getting off, Jerreon remained in his seat.

The transport continued on and the view opened. Rows of gleaming white boats of all sizes filled the bay. On the far side there were larger gray ships that filled him with wonder, boosting his attention, as did the sight of an airship that seemed to drop down and land in the midst of the buildings. It enthralled him, keeping his eyes open so he could see more.

The bus continued on, curving around the bay, until they pulled up in front of another set of buildings. These were not nearly as tall. Lush green grass carpeted the area giving it a garden-like feel that reminded him of his home, as it was also more open and airy. Kallie and Melissa both stood along with about half the remaining people on the transport. He rose.

Melissa glared at him.

"I will see you safely to your room," he said.

"I don't think that will be necessary," Melissa answered before Kallie could. "You need to go find your hotel." The warning came loud and clear.

When Kallie began to object, Melissa took her arm. "If you want to give him your number, he can call you, but he has been around you enough for one day. You need time to think things through." Melissa gave him a look that dared him to challenge the wisdom of her words.

"She is right. You need time. I will find you later."

"I'll only be here three more days," Kallie said.

"That is good. The farther you are from Lysias, the better. I will be close if you need me," he restated his promise from earlier. Unable to resist, he reached up and touched her cheek in a caress that he felt to his soul. "Have a good evening and sleep well."

He watched as they got off. Kallie looked back at him before disappearing down the trail the led to her room. Jerreon remained standing as the transport started to move. When it reached the edge of the complex, he walked forward to stop the driver. He stepped to the ground giving a final urge that the rest of the people forget all about him as he straightened.

The bus pulled away leaving Jerreon wondering what to do now. All he'd learned the last few days seemed useless here. Evidently, they let rooms. Jerreon figured the first thing to do was to obtain one. He just hoped he had enough currency, or that he could exchange it.

He walked back toward where they originally stopped for the people to disembark. He was drawing near when a car passed him and halted, letting a man and a woman out. The man got a large bag out of the back storage area of the car.

Jerreon followed them inside, studying their interaction with a woman at a long desk. When the woman at the desk finished talking with the man, she motioned for another man to come forward, who picked up the bag and led the man and woman out.

"May I help you?" The woman turned her attention on him.

"Yes, I would like a room please."

"Do you have a reservation?"

He shook his head. The actions continued as how it had with the other couple until they got to how to pay for it. He pulled out a coin from his pocket that, when he showed it to the last person, he had almost been robbed for.

"I haven't had time to exchange this yet. He laid it on the counter and reached out with his mind to gauge the woman's reaction. What he felt was skepticism.

"What is that?"

"A Stater."

"I can't take that." She frowned at him.

"What about a daric?"

"I've never heard of that either, but that thing looks old. I think you would have to take it to a coin dealer." *If it's real.* He picked up the words in her mind. The woman pulled back a little. "Don't you have a credit card?"

Jerreon wanted to say he'd never heard of that. Instead, he said, "thank you," then pushed out again with his mind, this time for her to forget.

He walked out the door, standing for a moment, wondering what to do before taking the path Kallie had.

The sun dipped low, touching the ocean. He passed a pool with a man and three children playing in the water.

What a blessing. He wondered if he and Kallie would have children. Was he to have a life here on this world? He could only hope. He would gladly forgo returning to his world to have a life with Kallie. What would she think if she knew his thoughts? More importantly what would she think if she knew he wasn't from this world? He had to tell her, but how?

Jerreon circled the pool and passed another building, then felt her presence. She was thinking of him. She was worried about him. He could feel her concern. It soothed him. He wanted to go to her but it wasn't to be, not yet. He needed to get rid of Lysias, then he could court her. Before that though, he needed to figure out how to fit into her world.

Sinking down on a chair by the pool, he looked over the small outdoor sitting area to her room. The curtains were drawn, keeping her from his sight, but nothing kept her from his mind. He started to lean back then sat up removing the pack so it would be more comfortable. Tonight he could relax. It should take Lysias a couple days to find them, and by then, Kallie would be headed to her home far away from there. He hoped it was far enough away.

The sound of splashing drew his attention back to the pool. It looked welcoming. As he watched, a woman came to the edge of the pool, and with some coaxing, the children got out with the father carrying one young boy. They stopped by a wall on one side and water came on and they cleansed off. He wondered why they needed to after just getting out of the water. They took sheets from a stack and dried off.

When they walked away, Jerreon stood and went to the wall. It only took turning one of the knobs to get water to flow, but what really beckoned him though was the pool. Removing his clothes down to his under garments, which were similar to how the man was dressed, he went down the steps into the water.

It was bliss. After the hot, dirty days with only the ocean water to clean off, it felt amazing. Though there was something in the water that smelled odd and made his eyes sting, so he kept his head up as he let his arms pull him through it in long, muscle loosening, strokes.

It didn't take him long to tire as he was already exhausted. He got out, going to the wall and started the water again. This felt fresher as he washed himself. Stopping the water, he picked up one of the sheetings. It was thick and soft. He dried himself off then returned to the chair to finish drying while he ate one of the last energy meals from his pack.

He had to figure out how to get currency soon, because he was running out of food, but he was too tired to worry about it then. He dressed and drew his jacket from the pack and pulled it on. It was not cold, but by morning it might be needed.

Leaning back, he placed his pack under his head for a rest and went to sleep.

CXEO

"Kallie, please tell me you're going to be careful," Melissa said coming out of the bathroom with her makeup bag.

"Quit worrying. He's gone." Even as she said the words, she knew they weren't true. Jerreon was somewhere close. Kallie didn't know how she knew it, but she did. "He didn't even get my phone number." She added to ease her friend. Melissa had enough to worry about. She took a pair of pants off the hanger and put them in the suitcase.

As soon as they walked into their room, Melissa's phone started ringing. Her daughter, Joy, was in labor two weeks early with Melissa's first grandchild. Luckily, Melissa was able to change her flight, but she had to hurry to make it to the airport on time.

"Well, I'm worried." Melissa reached out and caught Kallie's arm. "You're like one of my daughters."

"Don't worry. I'm fine," Kallie reassured. "Go see your new grandson."

Melissa brightened then glanced at her. "You will be careful?"

"Melissa! Honestly, what did you think of Jerreon?"

The older woman stopped in the middle of the room. "That's the problem. I like him a lot, and I don't know why. The last man I felt that good about right off, I married."

"See." Kallie smiled.

"I know, it's just I couldn't find out anything on him. There wasn't even a comment out there by a guy with that name, and I tried several different spellings. Do you know how uncommon that is? It's odd. There at least should have been something."

"He's from a different country," Kallie pointed out.

"Yes, but he didn't say which. Did you notice that? Maybe he's a terrorist. Maybe he's using you as cover."

"I see where your next story is going."

"It's pretty good, isn't it?" Melissa looked at her and crinkled her nose, then put her hands to her cheeks. "I've got to go. I can't believe it, me a grandmother."

Kallie zipped closed the suitcase and picked it up. "The shuttle ought to be out there now. They said they'd send it right over."

Melissa grabbed her purse and her computer bag and headed for the door. Kallie opened it just as a shuttle pulled up. The man got out and came to get the bag.

"It's been so fun. Come see me before you start a new job." Melissa hugged her.

"I'll try. Keep me informed on the baby."

"You keep me informed on the hunk. Something tells me you will be seeing him again."

Kallie wasn't going to deny it, because she not only hoped, but felt it was true. "I'll keep in touch."

Melissa got on the shuttle and Kallie watched it pull away. She thought about taking a walk instead of going back to her room then disregarded it, knowing what she really was thinking of doing was trying to find Jerreon. So, she went inside to get some writing done before bed. The only problem was, the hero in her story kept shifting to an extremely tall, well-built man, with white-blond hair and an accent that made women swoon. Finally, she gave up, knowing she wasn't going to do justice to her book and went to bed.

CB&O

"My One." The words drifted into Kallie's dream followed with the image of Jerreon. His finger stroked over her cheek, making her heart pound. The sun made his hair gleam like a halo around his head as he leaned over her.

Warmth and contentment filled her. "You make that sound like you love me."

"I do."

"But you said them before we'd even met."

"I have loved you forever. I was meant to find you."

Kallie looked in his eyes and saw the truth behind the words. "That sounds so mysterious."

"It is not. It is just meant to be. Do you not feel it – the bond – the connection between us?" His finger brushed her cheek again.

"Yes, but I don't understand it. I don't understand any of this."

"Yes, you do. You just have to look with your heart. It will tell you all your answers. You just have to accept them." He cupped her cheek in his hand.

"What would you have me do?"

"Trust me. Be patient. I was not planning on finding you now. I am not sure what to do about it because I am duty bound to complete what I came to do. Can you be patient?" His eyes searched her face for her answer.

"Yes, but maybe it is that I am to help you."

"To help me could be dangerous to you. I will not have that. I would rather never have you then put you in danger."

"Yet you say it was destiny that we found each other. And if it is, here at this time and place, then is it not destiny that I help you?"

He frowned. *"Your mind sees things in ways I wish you would not."*

She laughed at the perplexity in him. He stared at her and his head descended. *"My One."* His lips were a breath away when a ping penetrated her dream pulling her out.

Kallie stretched and looked around the room. Soft light filtered in around the curtains. Her thoughts went immediately to Jerreon. Had she dreamed him? Panic hit her, then eased. No, she could feel him, there on the edges of her mind. He was real.

There was another ping. Kallie looked over at the nightstand to her phone. She picked it up and opened the text message.

'He came at 5:24. Isn't he beautiful?'

There were two pictures attached, one of a crying infant and another of him asleep in Melissa's arms.

'He is. Congratulations.' She sent back a message then stretched again her thoughts back on Jerreon. She smiled. He was close. She tried to picture him but instead of any of the ways she'd seen him the day before, she got the image of him sleeping with shrubbery around him and a pool.

Kallie slipped from the bed going to the sliding glass doors to push the curtain aside. She saw him even before she stepped out on the patio. He lay asleep on a chaise lounge not thirty feet from her door. The sun hadn't quite reached him, but he seemed to glow without it.

The grass was damp on her bare feet as she crossed to him. A slight chill touched the air, but she was comfortable enough in the shorts and tank which she'd slept in. Kallie didn't really care who saw her. Her attention was focused on the man that, in less than twenty-four hours, had taken over her mind – and her heart.

His features hadn't softened much in sleep, and they were definitely no less striking. Adonis, as one of the sisters had called him, was fitting. He was dressed the same as he'd been the day before but had added a jacket that matched his pants.

She locked on his face. Her finger tingled with the thought of tracing the chiseled line of his jaw. She realized there was no stubble there and was surprised.

Kallie eased down on the cushion beside him. Drawn to follow her thoughts, she touched his cheek, similar to how he had in her dream. Her finger glided over the smooth skin. She traced down then back up his chin to his lips. They parted at her touch and curved slightly.

"*Kallie.*" She heard her name but his lips didn't move. Still, when she shifted her gaze she found him looking at her, his eyelids still half-closed with sleep. He moved his head and kissed her fingertip.

"I would wake like this every morning of my life." His words came low and rumbled as a hand slid around her waist.

She moved with just a slight amount of pressure to lean down.

"Soon, when it is right, you will be mine. Until then, I ask for just a taste to get to know you," he said just before their lips touched.

Heat and rightness swept through Kallie so strong the world dropped away, and there was only Jerreon. The kiss lingered only a second to know the truth. She was his and he was hers. Destiny had forged whatever bond was needed.

"Yes," he said, easing her back. "You will be a temptation for me until it is time."

"And when will that be?"

"Soon." He touched her cheek with reverence.

Kallie realized that was how he'd been doing it from the first. It seemed to have special meaning to him, and she liked it.

He smiled and looked over her. "You are as beautiful as your name says. Did you sleep well?"

"Yes. And you slept out here? I thought you were going to get a room."

"I tried but the woman hostel keeper could not accept my currency. I need to take it to get it exchanged."

"I'm surprised you were allowed to stay out here."

"A man came by once. He thought I must have had a disagreement with my wife. I let him think that and urged him to accept it was okay that I was here."

"Oh, so today, am I going to be the wife you were fighting with?"

"He will not remember." Jerreon's gaze dipped as if he'd just noticed the necklace she still wore. He reached up and touched the crystal. "We may not always be in agreement, but we will never fight."

"Oh, really?" She laughed at the sincerity in his words.

He nodded. "It is not in you. You are a peacemaker and have much love."

She was surprised by his assessment, especially because he was right, she really was a peacemaker.

His next words surprised her more. "I would never want to hurt you."

She swallowed, looking away. "I'm still surprised he let you stay."

"I urged it to be so."

"Okay." Kallie wasn't quite sure what to make of that. She didn't think it meant he threatened him, but wasn't sure what he could've said to persuade the security guard. She decided to let it drop. "So, what are your plans today?"

"First, I am hungry, so I must exchange my currency. How do I find a coin collector?" His brow furrowed slightly over the word.

"A coin collector?"

"Yes, the woman at the desk said I must have one of them to exchange my currency."

"There must have been some kind of misunderstanding. I'll help you do an exchange later. It's pretty early. I'll treat you to breakfast."

"What does it mean to treat me?"

"I will pay."

"I have currency." He stiffened.

"I understand," she soothed him. "We can exchange your money later."

"I also need to get some different clothes." He looked at her. His gaze heated.

"I ..." Kallie stumbled over what to say. "I didn't think about coming out."

"You came to me."

Kallie felt flustered. It was true. She'd just seen him there and came. She was decently attired, but still she flushed, because she obviously was wearing what she'd slept in. She hadn't even brushed her hair. Automatically, she reached up to smooth down the wild strands.

"I need to go in and change." She rose quickly, stumbling slightly. "Will you be all right here?" she asked, backing away before she did anything foolish, like asking him in while she changed. Melissa's warning of caution played over in her mind.

"Yes. I washed off last night." He pointed to the outdoor shower.

"I'll try not to be long."

"There is no hurry this day. I will swim while I wait."

"There's a changing room over there." She motioned to a door with a symbol of a man on it.

"Yes, I found it last night. Thank you."

"I'll be right back." Kallie turned and fled before she could invite him into her room, not quite sure how he would take the invitation. Though she was drawn to him, he was a stranger, even if he talked as if they were already married. She should stop that. It should terrify her, especially after her ex-boss and his possessive games, but for some reason, it didn't. With Jerreon, it felt too right.

Kallie hurried into the shower. She told herself she was not falling for him just because he was so good looking and had such a sweet accent. Which was the truth, neither of those things were what drew her, even at first. Yes, she'd noticed his looks, and she loved his height and the way he made her feel next to him. It was an oddity for her.

A lot of guys wanted the small, delicate women that made them feel big and strong, and she was definitely not that. Guys tended to let her open her own doors. She sighed, wondering if Jerreon would open doors for her. Sure, she could do it herself, but every once in a while, it would be nice to be treated like a lady.

Out of the shower, Kallie pulled on a pair of white capris with a bright blue-colored, short sleeve peasant shirt, and flat white sandals. She wished she had some high heels, but these went good with the outfit and were comfortable to walk in. She hadn't removed the necklace so she just added a pair of silver Celtic knot earrings.

Drying her hair, she ran her brush through it, letting it hang free in a thick blonde curtain that she knew a lot of guys liked. She thought Jerreon would be one who appreciated it. She fiddled with a touch of makeup, sprayed on her perfume, which had a light natural scent, then grabbed her purse and phone and went out the front door.

Kallie came around the building and froze. Jerreon stood by the showers, his back to her, running a towel down his long legs. He wore pale blue bottoms that were totally decent but, at his height, they showed a lot of tanned skin and corded muscles. He turned as if sensing her there and her mouth went dry. Adonis meets Hercules, the thought went through her mind. She knew he was muscled, but she'd never seen such a beautiful man. He wasn't bulgy just – perfect.

His eyes landed on her and he smiled. "You are beautiful."

"That's what I was thinking."

He frowned. "I am but a man."

"Yeah."

"Men are not beautiful."

"I," she drew it out, "could argue that with you right now."

"You find me so?" He let the towel drop, standing tall.

"Very." She breathed out, walking to him.

"Then this is good." He dipped his head. "I will dress then we can go eat." He reached for his pants and started to pull them on.

"There isn't a hurry. We can wait for your shorts to dry."

"It is not necessary, they hold no moisture."

She realized it was true. They seemed to be totally dry. "What an odd material. What is it?"

He looked down in thought. "Lysill. I do not know in your world."

"Is your shirt the same material?"

"It is made the same but different."

"I like the feel of it." She reached to touch the shirt as he pulled it down over his chest, then pulled her hand back. "Sorry." Heat flooded her cheeks. *What had she'd been thinking?*

"No concern." He caught her fingers in his hand and brought them to his chest as he eased toward her. The softness of his shirt didn't hold her attention as much as the warmth under it.

"My One." This time the words were said out loud as his other hand touched her cheek. He tipped her head up to meet his gaze. "I would kiss you, if you are accepting?"

Her heart pounded at his words. She raised and lowered her head in answer as his head dipped. He paused, just a breath away from her lips, as if giving her one last chance to pull back, then he brushed his mouth lightly over hers.

A sound like a groan rumbled out from deep within him.

"Jerreon." His name escaped her in response and his mouth lowered again, settling in firmly, savoring and taking her by storm. Kallie clung and accepted. Giving herself back in answer to the simple meeting of their lips, that was the promise of her heart.

The hand that caressed her cheek drifted back to cradle her head, tilting her to give him better access. The kiss remained tender, but left her trembling when he ended the kiss.

Jerreon ran his gaze over her face, then wrapped his arms around her, tucking her into him. Kallie dropped her head to his chest as her arms circled his waist. She managed a breath that filled her lungs with his musky scent. She knew him.

Chapter Six

Jerreon held his heart in his arms. He wished he never had to release her. Again, it was not time, but she gave him something to work for. When he stepped into the Syndais, he thought his life would be over once he stopped Ptolemaios. He figured he would just have to find a place on this world to live out the end of his days until he passed on.

Now he had a reason to live. He would make himself a place in this world where they could have a future. He needed to learn of this world. He had even more reason to save it.

He released her. "Where do we go to eat?"

She laughed and took his hand, leading him to the path.

"Isn't Melissa joining us?" he asked, running his thumb over her knuckles, enjoying the contact.

"She had to fly home last night. Her daughter went into labor and had a baby boy this morning. Melissa sent me the picture of the baby."

"That is splendid."

She laughed again.

"Did I say something wrong?"

"No, it's just your choice of words sometimes."

"I …" He wasn't sure what to say, so shrugged. "I try."

"Your speech is very good. Did you learn English in school?"

"No, from a translator. I will get better with time, but it is still learning."

"It's still learning?"

"Assimilating. It picks up broadcast and spoken language and updates." He watched her to see how she was accepting his explanation.

"I didn't know they had programs that did that. That's amazing. You must be a quick study though."

"I have a lot to learn. Where is the food place?"

"The main building there. They have a buffet. I thought you might find it to be good. You can pick what you like and eat as much as you want."

Jerreon found it to be very good. Different from what he was used to, but better than what he'd been offered the last few days. He tried a little of everything and found the fruits, breads and meats especially to his liking.

They talked easily about their homes and jobs. He found it interesting that Kallie wrote books, though she seemed quite timid about it.

"I'm still a new author. I'm afraid it's just a dream that someone would actually want to read something I write."

"Do you like what you write?"

"Yes. I love writing. I don't think I could live without doing it."

"Then that is what's important."

"What about you. You said you were in security?"

"Yes. I was a Council guard. I was under direct authority of the Council." He leaned toward her over the table and explained his duties.

"It sounds like you were more like a policeman or FBI agent."

He waited for the full information. "Yes, very close, but I reported only to the High Council and handle their directives."

"So, they sent you after this Lysias."

"Yes. Lysias Ptolemaios. They issued the directive, but I would have come no matter what was decreed."

"What did he do?"

Jerreon thought how to answer, then went for the straight facts. If any on this world had the right to know, it was Kallie, for it could affect their life together. "He planned to take over the Council. He wanted to rule. When I discovered his plot–"

"You discovered?"

"Yes. As I said I was over Council security. Lysias was taken before the Council to be judged. He caused an explosion at the Council building so he could escape. He killed two of the Council and injured many, plus many more in his escape. Life holds no meaning to him. He wants only what he can get and sees that as everything."

"I hadn't heard any of this." She leaned closer laying her hand on his again. He liked that she did that, especially that it seemed without thought.

"It was recently. And the knowledge of it will not touch here, unless I fail."

"Why then?"

"Because I believe after being in your country and learning of it, he will come here to take over."

"I don't think that can happen."

Jerreon shook his head. "Do not discount Lysias. He can do things you cannot imagine. He is very strong and has no honor. He will use whatever means he must. But you are not to worry about him. I will see to Ptolemaios. Now, what did you have plans to do today?"

"I'll help you change your money, then we'll go shopping."

"I do not intend to take up your day. What was it you had planned?"

"Just relaxing and doing some writing."

"Then you shall have your time. If you'll just get me started in the right direction?" He stood.

She followed his motion. "There is a bank just down the beachfront. We should be able to do an exchange there. I don't know what kind of a rate you'll get."

"Whatever you think is best. I put myself in your charge."

They decided to walk, enjoying the warm morning sun. "This is beautiful here," he commented.

Kallie took over telling him what she knew about the city and the bay, pointing out the big ships. "Later we can tour the USS Midway if you'd like. It's a museum now. I haven't visited it yet but planned to."

"I would like to join you on it, but it may have to wait until I see to Lysias."

She swallowed and glanced out at the bay then back and pointed across the roadway. "There's a bank."

They stopped at the corner while cars sped past. When the red hand changed to the image of a man walking, they crossed the road and she led him into a building.

"All right let's see your money."

He reached in his pocket and pulled out several coins, placing them in her hand. She stared down at them, then up at him.

"Is it not enough? I have more."

"Like this?" Her voice trembled.

"Yes. Is something wrong?"

"Is this gold?"

"Yes. Can they not be used? I was told it would be of worth here. Gargeli usually knows these things."

"These look very old." Kallie seemed to have trouble getting the words out.

"I'm afraid they probably are. Is there something wrong with that? They are all I have."

She studied the coins for a moment then looked back up at him. "I think the woman was right, we'll need a coin dealer for these. Are you sure you want to sell them? They look like they are very valuable."

"They are for my use here."

"All right then, let's see about some coin dealers here in the city." She pulled a small palm-sized object out of her pocket. He leaned in and watched her use it. Information appeared on the screen, similar to the intel device on his wrist.

"There are several listed," she said. "One is close enough to walk, but the others we'll have to take a taxi."

"Then we walk if that is okay?"

"Here." Kallie handed him the coins, then led him out of the building. She fell silent as they walked while Jerreon studied the architecture of the buildings and the area.

"Jerreon, where are you from?"

He knew what she was asking but still not sure how to answer. He couldn't lie to her. Lying was not honorable and she was His One, so he had to be honest, but he was worried about telling her all. "The city I am from is called Lantis. It is the ruling city. It is a long way from here. I am sure you have never heard of it. My people do not leave it very often."

She looked at him. He knew she was trying to decide if she believed him.

"Why not?"

"Mainly, it is forbidden, except under special occasions."

"Why?"

"We were once a great race and spread out wide in our thirst for knowledge, but we let that hunger over-shadow what was right. Some of my ancestors put themselves above those they contacted. We meddled in things we should not, and in some places, a few set themselves up to be deity. Arrogance opened a way for foolishness. It took a disaster to bring us back to face the reality of what was happening. We almost destroyed your world and our own. There was much devastation. A large portion of our population was lost. It has taken a long time to rebuild what was destroyed, and we have learned to use caution in our explorations."

"What kind of destruction?"

He could feel her mind working as she processed what he said. "Great. It was long before my time, but there were earthquakes and volcanoes. The world almost tore itself apart. The waves of it affected many other places. Many links were lost. It was a hard lesson for us. One that cost sixty percent of our people and affected greatly those left. As I said, it took a long time to recuperate and those left are much wiser. Unfortunately, not all are."

"I … I've never heard of any of this."

"We did not want others to know. Our lesson was hard. We have tried to make sure it did not repeat itself. Too much information too fast can become a dangerous thing."

She became quiet as they walked. Finally, he couldn't take it and reached over to catch her hand. "What I have said troubles you."

She looked at their hands then up at him. "I don't know what to think. I believe what you say, and I'm not sure why. It sounds unreal. I also believe there is more you are not telling, or maybe I'm denying the knowledge to myself."

He stopped and she turned to him. "When it is right for you, you will." He touched her cheek. She leaned into his touch, her eyes closing. He slipped his arm around her, easing her into him. "Listen to your heart, My One. Know where it leads you is true."

She smiled. "You would laugh at what it was telling me."

He reached out with his mind and picked the thought from her. *An alien, and not the kind that just skipped over the border.* He decided not to pursue the thought. "So where is this coin collector?"

"It should be getting close." She looked at her device again. "Just up around the corner."

They turned on the next street.

She paused. "I don't think this is the place we want."

"Why is that?" He looked at the building, not overly impressed by what he was seeing, but also not knowing what it should be.

"This is a pawn shop."

"What is that?"

"It's a place that buys things."

"But that is what I want isn't it."

"They'll not pay you as much as they are worth. You need a serious collector. I guess since we are here we might as well check it out, but do not be in a hurry to sell the coins." She glanced at the building. "In fact, I would suggest you only show one coin. It will be enough."

"One coin?"

"Yes, if it's worth what I think it is."

"All right." Jerreon walked with her to a building with metal bars covering the windows. A metal gate was pushed back to allow access to the door, but he did not find it very welcoming. He opened the door, allowing Kallie to walk in front of him, then stopped in the doorway. An odd array of things was stacked around the room. A long glass case ran along one side. Kallie walked toward it. He followed, looking in the case.

First, he saw knives, then things he didn't know what they were. There were intel devices like Kallie's and jewelry. Finally, they reached where coins were. Nothing was like what he had, most looked to be silver. There were a few gold coins, but they were smaller, and he expected much newer.

They stood there several minutes before a man, slightly rounded around the middle, ambled over. He stared at Kallie, enthralled. "May I show you something, maybe some jewelry?"

"No, thank you."

The man turned to him when Kallie did. A solicitous smile slipped from his face. "May I help you?"

Jerreon pulled one of the coins from his pocket. "I wanted to sell this." His trans-chip pulled what he figured was a more apt word.

The man eyed it, then motioned for him to put it on a padded tray. He reached under the counter and brought out an object. Holding it to his eyes, he leaned over to study the coin. "Just a minute." His voice sounded a touch sharper. He went over and retrieved a book from the desk.

"Do you know where this is from?" he asked.

"It is Greek I believe."

The man thumbed through the book, looked at the coin, then back at the book. "How much do you want for it?" the man asked, he shifted side to side.

"What it is worth."

The man scowled slightly, raising a clinched fist to his chin, and tapped it against mouth. "I'd have to do some things to verify if it is real and not stolen."

Jerreon was surprised at the comment, then he caught an impulse from the man. Opening his senses, Jerreon probed out. It wasn't hard to read the man's thoughts, they were so strong.

"If that's real, it's worth a fortune. Even if the coins not old, it was worth a lot, but I bet it is. And the guy doesn't have any idea what he has. The boss would never need to know." The man shifted a little, glancing at Kallie. *"He's probably trying to impress the gorgeous blonde. Or at least get lucky. I'd like to get lucky with her myself, but that would never happen.* "I can give you three hundred for the gold that's in it."

Jerreon didn't need to have Kallie's touch on his arm to know it wasn't a good offer. "No, thanks." He reached down to pick up the coin, knowing the man wasn't going to be honest with him.

The man dropped his hand over his. "Four hundred. That's all I can go without any proof of authenticity."

Jerreon picked up the coin.

"Hey." The man held his hand down. "Give me a minute to makes some calls to see if I can do better."

He pulled out a device similar to the one Kallie had. "Hey, I got a gold coin here. Looks pretty old." He listened a minute. "Yeah, okay."

He put the device down. "Sorry man. Five hundred's all I can go."

Jerreon looked at Kallie. She shook her head in agreement with what he already concluded. "No, thank you." Jerreon slid the coin back in his pocket, then held his hand out to Kallie."

"You sure you don't want to reconsider."

"No, thanks."

"Can I interest you in something else?" he pressed coming around the counter.

Two men walked in the door, their gaze going to Kallie with obvious interest. She must have picked it up because she reached out to take his hand, easing close. When the men's gazes went to him, there was menace followed by calculation.

Jerreon wished Kallie wasn't there. He did not like the feeling of malice he was getting, even when they turned their attention on a stack of wheels beside the door. There was danger.

"Do you have the number for a taxi?" She turned back to the man by the counter.

He shook his head. "You should be able to get one at the corner. They go by there all the time."

Jerreon squeezed her fingers in reassurance as they walked out, heading to where the two roads crossed. A large man wearing a black T-shirt stretched taut over bulging muscles leaned against the corner of the building. There was another man who was much shorter than Kallie walking toward them from the corner. They were the only two people in view on the street.

Prickles of warning skittered up Jerreon's spine.

"I don't like this." Kallie leaned into him.

He wondered if he was picking up her nerves, or if she his, or if they both were sensing danger. He didn't have time to figure it out. The man walking reached them just as they drew up in line with the man leaning on the building. The walking man shifted at the last second stepping in front of them, pulling a knife.

"Down the alley," he ordered.

The other man stepped away from the wall, moving in behind him. "Do what he says. We just want your money. No reason to get hurt."

"I have no money." Jerreon eased Kallie behind him and released her arm. She stepped back giving him space, but it put her in the alley.

"You just came from the shop. You must have somethin'," the smaller man said. He closed in, waving his blade tip around. "You're a big man, but this here pricker's real sharp. I'd hate to see anything happen to such a pretty woman. She's fine. If you want her to stay that way, hand over the wallet."

"I have no wallet."

"Then what's in your pocket and pack will do."

Jerreon stepped back as the big man stepped closer to Kallie. He knew he was being herded but was not quite ready to make his stance yet, then he heard a noise in the alley behind him. He didn't look, but probed out with his mind, contacting the other two men who had come into the shop. All were accounted for now.

He heard Kallie gasp but forced his focus from her. She was safe. They would have to go through him to get to her, and he would not let that happen.

"Give over what we want or we'll take the nice piece of flesh too." A voice rumbled from one of the men in the alley.

"I will give you a warning," Jerreon said calmly. "This is not what you want to do. It will bring you to no good end." He kept his tone low and urged them to listen and obey.

One of the men behind him pulled back as did the big guy in front, but their actions annoyed the man with the knife.

"What are you doing you idiots? Get him." He sprang forward, slashing out with the knife.

Chapter Seven

Jerreon spun to the side as the blade whipped by, barely missing his stomach. He pivoted, slashing his hand into the man. The blow knocked the man off his feet and to the ground. Behind, one of the men charged. Jerreon continued his motion around smashing his fist into the man. The man dropped to the ground snapping the other two from the stupor they'd drifted in.

Jerreon blocked a blow from one, while the bigger man grabbed him from behind, attempting to pin his arms down.

Kallie screamed.

"Stay back." Jerreon growled as he powered his arms up.

The man in front landed a punch to his side, then shook his hand. Jerreon pulled his legs up, putting all his weight on the big man holding him. Jerreon kicked out catching the man square in the chest, knocking him across the alley into a garbage receptacle.

Tightening his stomach muscles, Jerreon pulled the man holding him forward. The moment Jerreon's legs touched the ground, he grabbed one of the man's arms, dragging him forward over his shoulder, throwing him down onto an old car. The man groaned and fell still.

Jerreon looked around but none of the men were rising. He spun at the sound of movement and opened his arm in time to catch Kallie against him.

"Are you all right?" She ran her hands over his chest.

He caught one hand bringing it to his lips.

"I am well, but I think we better leave here."

She nodded, though her gaze still ran over him. He wrapped an arm around her and drew her out on the street.

She glanced back at the alley while matching her stride to his. "We ought to call the police."

"I cannot be entangled in your laws of the land. Hopefully they suffer enough for their attempt. One has a broken nose. Another, two ribs are broken and his hand. The other two will feel the effects for days."

"I think the guy in the pawn shop was behind it."

"I believe you are correct, but do not worry, his friends will see to him."

"Why do you say that?" She looked up at him.

"Because I urged the blame on him. They will remember it."

They made it to the end on the next block that crossed a busier road before they were able to flag down a cab. Kallie gave the address for another coin dealer, which sounded like he handled only coins and had a large number of good reviews.

"You can go back to the hostel if you'd like," Jerreon said.

Her lips twitched with a smile. "Hotel. Or, actually they refer to it as a resort. And no, I'm staying with you."

He squeezed her hand before bringing it to his lips. "I have to figure out your world if I'm going to survive in it."

"And I will help you."

He liked the firmness in her voice. It spoke of that she was with him in all ways. "I do not like you in danger." He kissed the inside of her wrist. He felt her heart leap.

She swallowed, her eyes locking on his. "You know, I've never been mugged before. And now in two days I've been in two attempts."

He frowned at that, figuring out her "mugged" meant being attacked. "I do not like to think I brought you danger." He released her hand, pulling back in the seat.

Kallie reached out, her hands framed his face and she turned his head to face her. "You did not. You kept me safe. Both times. And the first time you didn't know me." She leaned in and kissed him lightly.

It was briefly there and gone but the taste of her flowed through him. "I knew you from the moment I saw you." He touched her cheek. "As you knew me." He made it a statement and waited for her to disagree. She didn't.

"I don't know if I believe in love at first sight, but I believe in you."

He cupped her cheek and brought his mouth to hers hoping she always would. When she came to accept who he really was, it would take all her faith to believe in him and want to be one with him, because no matter their similarities, he was still an alien to her.

He let the kiss linger, though he was aware of the man in front driving the car. He broke the kiss, holding her to his side with one arm while wrapping her hand in his, holding it to his heart.

It wasn't long until they pulled up in front of another building. This one looked much nicer. It was tall, going up several floors with gleaming windows that reflected back the surrounding buildings. They got out and Kallie handed the driver some paper. Before she closed her purse, he took a piece of the paper from her.

He studied it. "This is what I need? Your money."

"Yes."

"The ore of the other seems more valuable than paper." He felt confused.

"It is. The government backs up the value of the paper with gold."

"Then why not just carry gold?"

"Good question. One hard to explain, other than it is just not done. What do you use where you are from?"

"We receive credits for our labor. Everyone serves in some capacity." He handed the paper back to her.

"We have credit cards. That is what people mainly use so they don't have to carry too much cash with them. We might want to do that for you. It would be safer and easier in most cases."

"The woman mentioned this last night when I went to get a room. If it is possible, I would do this."

"We'll see if it's possible. I'm surprised you don't have one to travel."

"It was not needed." He opened the door for her as they reached it and waited for a man to hurry out before stepping through.

She was by a board with writing when he entered. "The coin dealer is on the third floor."

Beside her, doors slid open and she stepped in. He followed and realized they were in a lift. When the doors opened again, she led him across the hall. Through the glass in the wall he could see display cases lining all the way around the room, but unlike the other place, these gleamed under bright lights.

There was a chime when they entered, and older man appeared out of a doorway. He smiled friendly.

"Hello." He held out his hand to shake theirs. "I'm Lynn Butler. Butler Coins."

Jerreon got a good feeling from him in the contact.

"Can I show you something?"

"Your site said you buy coins," Kallie said.

"Yes. I'll try to give you a fair price," the man said. "What do you have?"

Jerreon pulled his hand out of his pocket, holding out one of the coins.

"Oh my. Just a moment." He pulled a pair of white gloves from his pocket and put them on before reaching out to take the coin. "Oh my, a gold Stater. Isn't it beautiful? May I?" He motioned to an object on the counter.

"Certainly," Jerreon said.

Lynn Butler was already moving to place it on a tray, then moving the tray under the object, he looking down.

"It is beautiful. I'd say it's never been cleaned and looks in perfect condition. Roaring lion head. Double square." He looked up. "You wish to sell it?"

"Yes, and several others." Jerreon brought several more from his pocket.

Kallie moved in closer to see. Though she'd looked at them briefly at the bank, she really hadn't studied them close. Now, under the bright lights, she was stunned by their clarity. The edges were not precisely round like coins she was used to. These were punched blobs of gold. She would bet hand punched at that. A couple had sides that showed what looked like two squares, like a pair of dice. Some had a roaring lion's head and a couple had what looked like a lion and bull facing each other.

"Oh," Mr. Butler breathed out again. He looked about to faint. His fingers trembled as he lifted one with a bull and lion. "Croesus, 500 BC."

That shocked her. She glanced at Jerreon, but he made no reaction. *500 BC, could that be right?* She looked again at the coins. *O boy.* Her breathing sped up. She suddenly felt very nervous, like she'd never had around Jerreon. *Where did he get them?*

The thought must have come to Mr. Butler because he repeated her question almost word for word.

"May I ask where you got them?"

"They have been with my people for a very long time," Jerreon said in his way of answering and still being vague.

"Are you certain you want to sell them?"

"Yes. I need to, to live on. What I sell is depending on their worth."

"Quite a bit. They are spectacular. Though they will need to be authenticated."

"How long will that take?" Jerreon's brow creased slightly.

"It depends. I can't begin to do it. I apologize. I don't handle anything like these. As you can see, he motioned to the cases. "I specialize in American coins now, though I am tempted to get one for myself, for personal reasons. Though it would fit nowhere in my collection, and my wife would have a fit."

"Then you can't help us?" Kallie asked.

"Actually, I might be able to. There is a man that has an estate here, who does collect them and he would also be able to authenticate them himself. If he happens to be here, he is who you should talk to. He would probably be willing to buy them all. Let me see if I can reach him." He went over and looked through an old type card holder until he found what he was looking for, then took out his cell phone and dialed the number.

He was on hold only a moment before someone came on line. "Adam, yes. Fine, thank you, and you? Good. Why I called is, I have a man here interested in selling some King of Lydia Staters. Astonishing. I would say AU. Looks like ten, but I didn't ask."

Mr. Butler looked at them. "When would you like to meet him?"

Jerreon looked at her.

"Anytime," she said. "The sooner the better. How long would it take to get there by taxi or should I rent a car?"

He related her comment in the phone, a minute later he hung up. "He's sending a car for you. It should be downstairs in about twenty minutes, if that's okay?"

Again, Jerreon looked to her waiting for her answer.

"How well do you know this man?" she asked.

"Quite well. His name is Adam Bacchus. He's a little older than I am. He is somewhat of a recluse. He likes his privacy. He lost his wife a long time ago, never remarried or had any children. Kind of eccentric, but I think most coin or antiquity collectors are. I include myself in that comment. I think you will find him honest, and if he likes what he sees, may be quite generous."

"May I ask you how much you think they're worth?" she asked.

"Certainly. I'm not an expert on Staters, but yours look extremely excellent and if anyone is an expert, it is Adam." He went and pulled out a book and thumbed through. "I would say in the area of twenty-five thousand would be a good starting place."

Kallie felt her stomach muscles tighten. "Is that for all or a piece?"

"A piece. You'll have to bargain that with Adam. I expect he will be fair if he wants them."

She nodded looking over at the number of coins Jerreon had. There was possibly a quarter of a million dollars sitting there. "How do we thank you? You're not even getting a commission on this."

The man smiled. "I like seeing coins go where they will be appreciated. Besides, I'm sure Adam will give me a finder's fee, if he's happy. He has also been good to support me in the past when he's wanted something I could obtain. So, I don't feel as if I am out anything. It was a pleasure just seeing them, but if you're ever in the market again, remember me."

"That's guaranteed."

"Good. I think it would be better if you wait up here. Can I get you something to drink?"

"Water would be wonderful," she said.

"For me also, please," Jerreon added.

Lynn stepped into the back room.

"I take this is a large amount?" he asked her.

"Yes. I was not expecting anything like that. Didn't you know their value?"

He shook his head. "I just hoped it would be enough to live on while I found Lysias."

"I would say that shouldn't be a problem."

Mr. Butler came back handing each of them a water bottle, then went to look at the coins again. "They are very beautiful."

Kallie took a drink, stepping up to him. "Are they really that old?"

"Yes, some of the first gold coins ever minted. The first coins for that matter. And look, the stamping is so clear you can make out the Phoenician lettering."

"It sounds like you do know a lot about them."

"Just enough to be slightly envious. Do you know much about coins?"

"I have a Morgan silver dollar my father gave me and a mercury dime."

"What is that?" Jerreon asked.

Mr. Butler pointed them out in the case. "Of course, the price all depends on the date and the grade. But you have a good place to start. They are both very pretty coins." His phone rang. He looked at the message. "Your ride is here."

"Thank you so much." Kallie shook his hand, then Jerreon did.

"Thank you."

"You're welcome. Good luck with Adam. He'll let you know if they are the real deal." The man didn't sound like he doubted it. He wrapped the coins in a cloth and handed them to Jerreon.

They got downstairs and found a limo waiting just outside the door. "I think that's maybe for us." She walked to the man standing next to the car. "Mr. Bacchus."

"I'm his driver, Edward." He opened the door.

"This is nice. Much different than the taxi," Jerreon said as he got in beside her.

She laughed. "It doesn't get much better. This is my first limo ride."

"Kallie, I think that it would be better if I took you back to the motel. I have put you in danger this day. It was never my intention to do so. I would feel better if I knew you were safe until this business is complete."

She started to shake her head to disagree.

"Please," he said before she could start. "I would do this. You wanted to write your book. I will be back as soon as I am done."

Kallie wanted to argue, but she could feel the importance of this to him, it almost seemed like it was something he had to prove to himself, though she wasn't sure why. Slowly she nodded. She leaned forward in the seat. "Edward, would it be possible to drop me off at my hotel first?"

"Of course." She gave the name and he detoured to the marina.

"Thank you for this." Jerreon touched her cheek. "I will find you there later. You will be there won't you?"

"Yes. I think I'll write by the pool." When they pulled up out front of the resort, she was tempted again to ask if he was certain. Instead, she got out of the car when the door was opened.

He followed her out. "I will come for you later. I believe I owe you a meal." He caught her hand and raised it to his lips.

"I'll be waiting."

He got back in, and the limo pulled away. She prayed for his safety, then headed for her room. Knowing the story she'd been working on was not going to get finished at this time, because she was starting a new one featuring a tall, white-blond hero. Maybe he'd be a coin dealer. She could call Mr. Butler for information. She was sure he would help her. No, he was a government agent after a terrorist.

ᏚᎮᏋᎧ

Jerreon glanced back to see Kallie standing there. He hated to leave her, but until he got the money problem settled he was not risking her being in danger. She said it was a great amount of money. The men who attacked them earlier knew of only one coin, what would happen when they found out how many he carried? What he had in his pocket that he showed the coin dealer was but a small portion.

He had detected no sign of malice in Lynn Butler or in the driver, Edward, but he was going to be prepared. He enjoyed the ride, listening to the soft music that filled the car. It wasn't long until they pulled up to a metal gate with scrolling and a roaring lions head, similar to that on the coins. The gate swung open automatically to let them pass. They stopped in front of a large white marble edifice. Two reclining lions sat on either side of the five steps up to the massive door.

Again, Edward got out and came around to open the door. Before Jerreon made it out of the car, the doors to the house opened and a silvered haired man with a mustache and a small beard came down the steps to greet him.

"Mr. Bacchus." Jerreon dipped his head in greeting.

"Yes. I'm afraid I didn't get your name from Lynn." He eyed him up and down.

Jerreon felt as if he was getting read much the same as he was doing to the man. "Jerreon Ander."

"Jerreon. Interesting name. Well, shall we go inside and see what you have for me?"

"Certainly."

"I thought Lynn said you had a woman with you?"

"We dropped her off at her hotel. She is an author and wanted to get some writing done."

"An author, really? What does she write?"

"She said romantic suspense. That it is about love, adventure, and heroes." *He hoped he got that right.*

"I see. Well, right this way to my study." Mr. Bacchus eyed him again curiously.

The house was large, open and airy with lots of light coming in. It reminded Jerreon of his own family home, though he had a smaller room not far from the Council building where many of the Council guards stayed to be close. That was gone now.

He looked around at the furnishings, finding the place very pleasing to his soul. Stepping into the study was like stepping into another world. Again, a large, open room, but this one was filled with treasures. Paintings lined the wall where there were not bookcases. Sculptures sat on pedestals. Display cases were scattered around the room. At a glance, it appeared some held jewelry and small ornaments, while others held coins.

It was easy to see the man had collected widely. The question was would he want more? Jerreon hoped he would want at least one. From what Kallie had expressed to him, one would be enough to keep him awhile. That would give him time to deal with Lysias, then he could find buyers for the others.

Adam Bacchus led him to a large desk that was already set to inspect the coins. The man pointed to a chair. "Please have a seat." He settled down. "May I see them?"

Jerreon removed his pack and put it on the floor. Bacchus watched the movement expectantly, then looked quite shocked when Jerreon pulled the coins from his pocket.

"I was not expecting that." Bacchus laughed until Jerreon released the coins. "Oh!" The man reached for one, easily more enthralled than the coin dealer had been. He fell silent, studying one then another.

He had an instrument on his desk similar to the one the coin dealer had, and several other devices. He put one of the coins in one.

"What is that?" Jerreon asked, interested in what he was doing.

"It will tell me the makeup of the gold. It is one of the fastest ways to weed out possible forgeries."

Jerreon nodded, watching with even more curiosity.

Bacchus started telling what he was doing, what he was looking for and going into greater depths as Jerreon showed himself a keen learner.

Finally, the old man turned to him. "I'll offer you three hundred and fifty thousand for them if you want to sell them all right now."

"That is considerably more than Mr. Butler said."

"They are worth it. They are all superior. There are none better in any museum. They are truly amazing. If you will give me your bank account number, I will have the money transferred immediately."

"Bank account?"

"Is there a problem?" Bacchus's eyes narrowed.

"I am not sure what that is." Jerreon decided to be truthful. "I was expecting currency."

"You cannot walk around with over a third of a million dollars on you. Then again, I guess you have been." He seemed to see humor in it.

"If you could help me make a call, I'm sure my," he hesitated, unsure of what the correct term he should use in reference to Kallie, "friend has this and she can help me."

"Are you certain?" Adam Bacchus pressed a finger to his lips, a scowl tightening his brows. "How long have you known this woman?"

"We met yesterday."

Skepticism peeked from the man, easy to read without even trying.

"I'm not sure that is wise."

It was Jerreon's turn to smile. "Thank you for your concern, but I can assure you Kallie is trustworthy."

The older man studied him. "You are a contradiction," he said after a moment.

"I do not understand. A disagreement?" Jerreon searched the translation for a clearer meaning, but Mr. Bacchus took over the explanation.

"More of a paradox. May I ask how you came upon them?" He motioned to the coins.

Mr. Bacchus eyed him looking for the truth and Jerreon gave it to him. "They have been with my people for a long time, and were given to me for my use here." Jerreon met his gaze.

"What is your purpose here?" he asked forthright.

"I am after a criminal from my land."

"He must have done something terrible for you to be given so much just to come after him." The man eyed him.

"He did, and if not stopped, he would do worse here."

"Really, what would that be?" There was a challenge in the question. As if he thought he wouldn't tell him.

"Set himself up to be a god."

Bacchus fell silent then looked him up and down one more time. "You are a man out of place. Aren't you?"

"I am not sure what you mean," Jerreon returned, meeting his gaze.

"That is the closest thing to an untruth I think you have said to me." The old man stood and walked around the room, coming to stop by a large mosaic globe made of inlaid pieces of rock. He laid a hand on it and turned it slightly, looking over at him. "Is it even possible that you can go home?"

Jerreon met his gaze, feeling the same kinship as he did to some of his old mentors. "No, my destiny is here now."

"With this woman, Kallie."

"Yes."

The man nodded and Jerreon got the impression he had made up his mind. "Well, you're going to need some help, more than I'm afraid your friend, the author, can give. I have a million questions to ask you, but we'll have to get to them later, as I doubt we have time for that."

"I have one for you. Where do you believe I am from?" Jerreon asked just as forthright.

"The exact location or what it is called, I have no idea. Some distant universe I suppose." He nodded to the coins. "This is not the first time your people," he used the term Jerreon had earlier, "have been here, but it is for you."

Jerreon nodded.

"First thing, we need to get you an ID, that is identification that we carry here, or do you have any?"

Jerreon shook his head.

"I actually know someone that might be able to help with that. And we'll need to get you a bank account. That, I can take care of." He picked up the phone and started to dial. "I think it should be an off shore account. It will be safer for right now. Less questions."

Adam turned his attention to the phone. "Yes, Raymond. Fine, but I need to have you help me with something. I wanted to set up an account for a distant relative. He is the last I have. The name is Jerreon Ander." He spelled it out. "Take three hundred and fifty thousand from my account to open it. We will be adding more to it later. For a password."

Adam looked over. "I need a word for you to access the account. One you won't forget and also several numbers to make it more secure."

"Lantis 3018," Jerreon said without hesitation.

Adam's eyebrow lifted but he just repeated it in the phone. "That's correct. You can send all the information here, and I will get you the other details later. Thank you." He hung up.

"He will start to process it on my clearance. You might as well start calling me Adam. You have now become my relative. A great-nephew or something like that, I think. We should receive all the information soon and I will teach you how to access the account. A phone will be helpful, but you might want to get a line tied to your friend's." He smiled but this time it was not as skeptical. "I have one you can use until then. I'll put my number in so you can reach me at any time. I don't suppose you know how to drive a car?"

Jerreon shook his head. "I have observed. It does not appear too difficult."

"Yes, we'll get to that, your ID should be our next priority."

"How can I thank you?"

He made a wave of his hand. "It is an old man's pleasure. Though, I wish you had more of those," he said it, wistfully looking at the coins.

"How many would you like?"

Adam turned back, straightening. "You have others?"

Jerreon reached down, lifted his pack and pulled out one of the fist sized pouches and dropped it on the table, followed by the other. "They are not all the same, but they are all gold."

"Oh my." Adam started to laugh. "I might as well transfer over a large portion of my fortune to you right now."

Chapter Eight

Kallie really did try to get back into writing the story she was working on, but couldn't. After a few minutes, she gave up and opened a new document and started the new story, but instead of a government agent, she ended with a tall, gorgeous alien chasing a criminal from his planet through space. The words tumbled out as she tried not to worry about Jerreon. After a couple hours, she stood and stretched.

She wished she could call him, or that he'd call her. She'd given him her phone number and explained to him that he could reach her with it. Kallie tried not to think about a phone being unfamiliar to him.

She looked at her computer and thought of her making him an alien. Was that what she truly believed? Reaching up, she fingered the crystal deciding not to ask questions she really didn't want the answers to. Falling in love with an alien, and not the type that just snuck across the border, didn't sound like a good idea.

The thought made her think of their crossing the border. She'd kept an eye on him when he went to talk to the security man. Jerreon had no passport, only the customs paper. Yet the man didn't even flinch in letting him through.

The ancient gold coins were easier to explain in her book than they were in real life. Was Jerreon all right? She should've insisted on going with him. He didn't seem at all familiar dealing with people, though he was savvy. He read people, almost like he read their thoughts.

My One. It echoed in her mind and her heart. Kallie couldn't discount it being real. It had been too strong, too true to her soul. She knew it was right. She wrapped a lock of hair around her finger and stopped the pacing that she'd been doing.

"Oh man, this can't be real. Where is he?" She looked out the window, wishing he'd appear. It had been a long time. *Was he all right?* Kallie repeated in her mind. She tried to soothe herself by bringing up the image of how easily he'd handled the four guys.

Kallie wished she'd asked more about the man he was going to meet. Mr. Butler trusted him, and it sounded like respected him, but she didn't know anything about Mr. Butler, besides the fact she actually liked the man, and he had a lot of good reviews online. But this was Jerreon's life she was concerned about. Kallie paced the room again. Jerreon felt comfortable with Mr. Butler too, and he'd sensed trouble immediately at the other place.

She should've insisted on going with him. Kallie groaned. She was back where she'd started. Giving up, she changed into her swimsuit and headed for the pool, taking her computer with her. At least she could get a tan while she worried.

There was only one older couple by the pool, lounging in the sun. Everyone else must still be off sightseeing. She didn't want to go anywhere until Jerreon returned. What if he didn't? What should she do? What could she do, was the better question?

"Stop! You're not going to start that again," Kallie said aloud, then looked to see if the older couple had heard. They didn't seem to be paying any attention to her. She put her stuff on a table under an umbrella then headed to the pool.

The warm water felt great on her skin. Stretching out, she let her arms pull her through the liquid comfort. She could get to love this. Sun, swimming, writing. What could be more perfect? Jerreon!

Kallie kicked harder and dug in with her arms. Twenty laps and she pulled up winded. Swimming wasn't an activity she was used to, but maybe she should add it to the other things she regularly did like hiking, going to the gym and playing volleyball.

Kallie eased back in the water just letting herself float when she felt him, a tingling awareness that filled her. She stood turning in the pool to see Jerreon. He walked across the lawn toward her. Heat spread through her body.

His eyes clung to her. He didn't look around, coming straight for her until he stopped at the edge of the pool and stared down.

Kallie knew her swimsuit was considered modest by most standards, but still it hugged her curves and showed a lot of skin. The heat she felt surged into a raging inferno that engulfed her to the point that it was amazing the water around her didn't start to steam.

Jerreon seemed to blow out a breath.

"Beautiful." The thought came to her and she blushed.

He held out his hand. Kallie walked the edge of the pool, caressed by his eyes as well as by the water.

She was conscious of him as she took each step. She caught the hand he extended and let him draw her up. The connection between them sizzled with promise.

His free hand came up to caress her cheek, then moved to burrow into her hair and tilt her chin up. He took her mouth with the fierceness of a conquering warrior, but she knew no fear. Never would he do her harm, but she felt weak and trembling when he broke from the kiss to pull her against him.

Kallie laid her head on his chest and just tried to breathe.

"I'm getting you wet." She finally managed to form words.

"It is of no consequence." He leaned his head back to look down at her, his other hand coming up to frame her face. "You were worried for me. I felt your fear. Never doubt I will come back to you."

"I …" She didn't know how to say she loved him. It was too soon. "Could you really feel my concern?"

"Your feelings are strong and they call for me. I will always be able to find you. We are one even if the union has not happened yet. My heart has accepted you."

"I've never had anyone talk to me like that before." She lowered her head back to his shoulder, listening to his heart.

"Does it scare you?" His hands ran over her back in strokes that were a cross between comforting and thrilling.

"Can you feel what I feel?"

"Yes, if I tried, I could read all, but I would rather you share with me. I would like the words."

Kallie raised her head and looked into his clear aqua eyes. "I feel no fear from you, but I do feel fear for you."

He kissed her forehead. "Have no fear. All is well."

"*For now.*" The words slipped into her mind. She didn't think they came from her, but a warning deep within. She forced them down and reached up to touch his face as he did. "Did he buy a coin than?"

"Adam bought several. He also has been a great help to me."

"Adam?"

"Yes. You will like him. Do not worry." He stroked her cheek. "Will you go change and take me shopping." He released her and went to pick up a towel from the stack. He came back and wrapped it around her. His lips twitched as he looked down at her. "I find you an appealing sight."

She blushed again. "There is nothing wrong with my bathing suit, in fact a one-piece is considered modest."

ALYSIA S. KNIGHT

"But there is nothing modest in your effect on me. You are very desirable. Which is not bad for one's own One. It is good you find me desirable also."

The confidence in his words struck her as funny. "Who said I did?"

"You did. It was in your thoughts earlier this day."

That he might actually have read her thoughts made her blush.

"Do you know at times color brightens your cheeks in a most becoming way?"

She ducked away. "Stop that." She held up her hand warding him off when he went to reach for her to pull her back. "Okay, we need ground rules set here."

He tipped his head to the side, and she got he was trying to understand what she meant. "No reading my thoughts. It is not fair."

"I do not try to read your thoughts. Just I hear some. They are so strong they come to me."

"Well, ignore them."

He laughed. "That is impossible, but I will try not to pry. Does that promise please you?"

Kallie figured that was the best she could get. "Yes," she conceded.

"You know, you have read my thoughts."

She swung back to him, ready to discount but something stopped her.

"Yes." He nodded. "You heard me call you 'My One' when I first saw you. You have heard me other times."

"I'm not sure."

"Yes, just think and you will know. You have trusted me even when you should not have." He kissed her cheek. "As the bond between us deepens, your ability will grow. For now, just close your eyes and concentrate on me."

He brushed his hand over her face, encouraging her lids down, her chin tilted up to him. "Come," he whispered.

"Do it. You can reach me." His fingers skimmed her brow. "That's it. Feel me here."

Warmth greeted her, love poured out to her stronger than she'd ever dreamed. She felt pride coming off him in what she did.

"Know me, My One."

The words reached her and she did. Kallie opened her eyes. "Is it the crystal?" She reached up and fingered the stone, searching his face for the answer.

"It might help, but you have to possess the ability first."

"How can that be?" Kallie felt slightly light-headed and a touch queasy.

He shrugged. "It may be, it just came out in you. Possibly your race is just starting to develop the ability. Or maybe …," He paused obviously in thought.

She waited a minute then touched his cheek, drawing his attention back to her. "Jerreon?"

"My people came here long ago. Though it was not to happen, we were a younger race and not as disciplined then, some of our people mated with people here." He brushed at her hair. "I wonder if it is possible we share some of the blood line. The strains of life are interesting on how they pull up traits in their own time."

Kallie was not sure what to think of what he said. And it went deeper. Jerreon had basically said he was not from her world. The thought should panic her, but didn't. She knew no fear of him. Deciding she wasn't ready for more, she pushed it away and went to the table.

He reached out and picked up her computer first. "Did you get much writing done?"

"A little. I started a new story."

"What kind of stories do you write?"

"About love and adventure." *About falling in love with an alien on a quest.* She glanced over to gage his reaction.

He made no reaction to hearing her thoughts. "These are good things." He watched as she slipped on her sandals. "Your toe nails are the colors of flowers."

"The color's pink, or I guess you could say rose. Do the women paint their nails where you come from?"

He shook his head. "I find them pretty." He walked with her into her room.

"I should probably try to get us a rental car. I'm not quite sure where to take you shopping."

"We have a car waiting. Adam has given it for our use. He also gave some suggestions of where to go. The first is his tailor to measure me for a suit and some shirts, then something called an outlet mall. He said you would know what that was."

"Yes. That was nice of him." She pulled a pale blue skirt out of her closet and a white top with a painted stylized flower on it. She wondered what this Adam was really like. Once again she had to remind herself Jerreon was a good judge of character.

She paused in the doorway to the bathroom. "Can you read this Adam's mind?"

"He is a complex man, but I can easily read impulses off him. There is nothing to fear from him."

She felt relieved in his reassurance. "I'll hurry."

"Take your time. Edward said he has some homework to keep him occupied. He is studying at the university here, but does not have any classes this day. May I use your computer? Adam showed me how to manipulate one."

"Sure." She fought to keep from laughing. "We need to work on your word choices." She started to close the bathroom door.

"Adam said the same thing. He has invited us to dine with him tonight."

She froze, looking back at him.

"He is as curious of you as you are of him. Go now." He motioned her away, one side of his mouth pulling up to show a dimple she hadn't noticed before, though how she missed it, she didn't know.

Kallie had to force herself to close the door. A dimple? She would never have thought and wondered if she could get one to show on the other side. She leaned back against the door, placing her hand over her heart. He really was gorgeous.

With a sigh, she peeled off her swimsuit. She was in the shower before it dawned on her he was waiting for her just on the other side of the door. Never in her life had she been in a hotel with a man before.

Hurriedly, she washed her hair, dried off and dressed. Jerreon was at her computer, totally engrossed when she came out. "What are you looking at?" she asked, coming up beside him, to see things scrolling over the screen.

"My ... computer." He tapped his wrist. "Is updating and storing knowledge of your world. I am learning of your government. Trying to figure how Lysias will try to take dominion over it. It is quite complex, though the preface of it was quite simple. I like your Declaration of Independence. Most intriguing." He shut down her computer and stood.

"Will you tell me about your government?" she asked, picking up her purse, letting him direct her to the door.

"If you would like. There is a Council of twenty-four. They are selfless individuals – learned, strong in talent and wise. Our laws have been set for ages." He led her to the waiting limo and opened the door for her.

Edward straightened in his seat and put down the tablet he'd been reading from. "You're to let me do that?" he said as they got in shaking his head in good humor.

"I was here and know how." Jerreon answered. "We are ready to go."

The tailor didn't take as long as Kallie thought. All he did was take measurements, show them several pictures of suits to see what styles were preferred in what he suggested would look good on Jerreon. He then said Mr. Bacchus had given a list of what he wanted for him and that he would take care of the bill.

That thought made Kallie a bit nervous, but she had no choice but to accept it. Still she wondered again about the man.

Edward took them to a big and tall shop that he found out about from one of the security guards that liked to shop there. The place had a surprisingly good selection and it wasn't long until they had a couple pair of slacks, jeans and shorts, a dozen casual shirts, swim trunks, T-shirts, underwear. At the mall they went to, he added dress shoes, loafers and gym shoes, which he liked a lot, and sunglasses.

"Do I have everything I need?" he asked as he helped her into the car again.

"I think so. I've never outfitted a man before. You might need a suitcase to haul it in."

"Adam has invited me to stay with him. Since we are not married, it would not do for me to stay with you."

Kallie's heart jumped at the word married.

He leaned forward to talk to the driver. "Edward, can we stop and take a walk on the beach?"

"Sure."

Jerreon stayed quiet as they drove which probably was a good thing because Kallie's mind was racing all over. It was only about fifteen minutes before Edward pulled the car over and stopped at a beautiful stretch of beach. People dotted the sand, but it was not overly crowded.

Jerreon got out and reached a hand back to her. Kallie looked at it feeling like destiny was taking over again, just like it had done the day before when Jerreon came to her rescue.

She hesitated then laid her hand in his, letting him pull her up to him.

Kallie looked into his eyes for a moment before he turned, leading her out onto the sand. Her hand remained in his and felt quite natural there. They walked down to where the water reached its peak on the sand.

He stood for a moment facing the ocean, then turned. Framing her face in his palms, he tilted her face up to him. "You should not be shocked when I talk of marriage, My One. You know my thoughts are for you forever."

Kallie knew she should say that it was too soon, but didn't want to. She wanted to believe in a forever with him.

"It is my wish also." He dipped his head to kiss her cheek. "I have learned that with your people this is not always so, but for mine, we mate only once. When we do, we give our heart and soul to that union. We pledge our all. That is what I offer you."

He tipped his head down to rest his forehead on hers. "I should and would have waited until I have dealt with Lysias, but I cannot. I have given up my home and I can accept this. But I cannot live without knowing I will be with you. I would give all for just one day with you." His gaze grew intense. "I do not know what we must do to be married on your world. Please tell me, if it can be done, that you will be mine."

There were only his eyes to see. They breathed in the same air. Their hearts aligned and beat as one.

"I love you." Kallie didn't have to think of the answer, it just came. "I will be your One as there is no other for me."

"As words spoke, we are One in my world. As soon as it can be made so, we will be One here. Is this acceptable to you?"

She nodded, emotions swelling over her so strong she couldn't get a word out, but it wasn't necessary. Her thoughts flowed.

"My One." He kissed her, then wrapped her in his arms.

Kallie slipped her arms around him and held on.

Just one day. Jerreon would face Lysias. Kallie had no delusion of Lysias's strength and viciousness. Would one day be all they would get? Would they even get that?

ር807

Jerreon knew Kallie's concern. He also knew her love. If he asked, she would come to him now, accepting his words that to his people they were married. It was the truth, but he would wait until they were married in the eyes of her people, too. As soon as he could, he would ask Adam to set in order what was needed. Once the man met Kallie, he would help.

He wanted to take her to meet Adam because if her fear did come to fruition, and something happened to him when he faced Lysias, he wanted Adam to see to her as he knew the man would. Maybe as soon as the ceremony could be completed, he should see if Adam could help him send her away somewhere safe until the confrontation with Lysias was over. She had said she was to leave in two more days which was good. He wanted to know she was far enough away not to be in danger from Lysias.

It might be wise if Adam went also. If Lysias found out he was helping, he would harm the man out of spite. It was the way Lysias was. No one was allowed to stand up to him. Jerreon knew that attitude gave him an advantage and time before Lysias spawned havoc on the world. Lysias would want to destroy him first for denouncing him and standing up to him at Lantis, then for coming here to stop him. Lysias would understand he had to stop him before he could get hold of this world.

Jerreon let that slip from his mind as he looked down into Kallie's eyes and felt her love. He tightened his arms and she rose to meet him, sliding her arms around his neck. Her lips were like nectar – an ambrosia he could never get his fill of. He drank fully, letting the headiness of her wash over him. He savored then eased her away while he still could.

"Come, My One." He led the way back to the limo.

He felt Kallie stiffen a few minutes later when the car pulled through the gates. "Wow, I guess I was expecting this, but wow. This mansion is something."

"You will like it. The pool and deck around it look out over the water. It is open and light. It reminds me of my home."

"You have not told me where you are from yet," she said pointedly.

"Yet you know, but I will tell you all later, for now let us enjoy it here." He brushed his lips over hers. When he shifted away, Kallie saw a very distinguished looking gentleman coming down the stairs, eliminating the chance for discussion.

Jerreon got out, going to the man to shake hands.

Kallie followed more slowly. The man might be old, but he seemed physically fit, and there was no dimming or disguising the sharp wit. Adam Bacchus was a man to be reckoned with if he chose to, and Kallie figured, quite often, when it was important to him, he chose to.

"Adam, may I introduce you to Kallie."

"My dear. It is a pleasure. I just spent the last hour reading the beginning of one of your novels. I have enjoyed it so far."

Surprised, Kallie looked at Jerreon, then back to him. "Thank you."

"Dinner is almost ready. It will be set up on the patio. I hope that is to your liking. It is my favorite place to dine. We should be in for a beautiful sunset tonight." He led the way through the house.

Kallie tried not to gape, but she found it stunning, from the marble tiled floor to the opulent ceiling with several layers of stacked moldings. It was a show piece, yet it still had a comfortable feel to it, especially when they stepped out on the patio. The pool, with aquamarine and cobalt tiles, glistened in the sunlight. Beyond it the view stretched out to the ocean as Jerreon had said. To one side Kallie caught sight of the corner of a tennis court.

"This is amazing. You have a beautiful home."

"It suits me well. May I ask, where are you from?"

Kallie got the impression he knew the answer and was just being polite. "I have a small apartment in Boise, Idaho. I've been living there for a couple years, but I'm thinking of moving. I left my job recently." She felt a flash of unease and pushed it away. "I'm hoping to be able to make enough writing to survive."

"What happened with your job?" Jerreon turned on her, his brow furrowed. Kallie felt her face heat and she glanced away. "You're peeking."

"I was not. You felt discomfort. What is it, My One?" He touched her chin, tipping it up to him.

"My boss started to do things I didn't like?"

"Such as?" Adam asked. There was a stiffening in the man.

"It was nothing I can prove." She looked to Adam and shrugged. "He used to stand behind me and watch me. I didn't think much about it. Then I started to miss things from my desk. I had a picture taken when I was hiking with some friends, then one taken at my first book signing. A couple other things, change missing from my drawer, my extra name badge.

"A month ago, he asked me out. It was more like a demand. I turned him down, saying I didn't date people from work. I thought that was reasonable as I never had before. He seemed to accept that but I started getting calls with no one there and the number blocked. Then he started to make comments about me going out with him again and that a woman needed a man in her life to protect her."

She shrugged. "As I said I have no proof he was the one doing anything. But I got a feeling that I had to get away before something did happen. I had the writer's conference coming up. I put it on the schedule months earlier. The only vacation I'd scheduled for the year. He came to me and said I couldn't go. He made several excuses. When I pressed, he blurted out it wasn't safe to be away from him. I turned in my two-week notice that afternoon."

"Can he do these things?" Jerreon took her hand, running his fingers over her knuckles.

"He shouldn't be able to," Adam answered. "But if he's sneaky enough, it happens." He looked at her and nodded.

Kallie got a sense of respect from him. She wondered if it was real or wishful thinking. After being around the man for just a couple minutes, she wanted his approval.

"While we're waiting for dinner, why don't I show you my collection? I have your coins on display now, if you'd like to see?" He led the way through another set of doors that went right into his study.

They wandered around the room while he told them about the items he had on display, until a woman appeared at the door.

"Dinner is ready to be served.

"We'll be right out." He turned back to them. "You would probably like to freshen up first." He directed the comment to Kallie.

"Yes, please." Kallie took her cue and went into the restroom as Adam Bacchus ushered Jerreon on to continue their conversation. Once again it was hard not to be impressed by the mansion, but Kallie was more interested in what was being said in the other room. She knew the conversation was going to be about her. The question was, would it be favorable?

She was nervous. This must be what it felt like to meet the in-laws. Though, she figured she would never truly get to meet Jerreon's. What family had he left behind? Her parents were older, but they were the best. She had Dillon, her older brother, who was taking over the family farm. He was always there for her if she needed him, even though he was married and had two kids. She tried to get back to visit every couple months. It would be so hard to know they weren't there.

The need to see Jerreon swept over her. Washing her hands, she hurried out to find him.

ᏨᎡᏲᏅ

"You are right. I like your young woman," Adam said as soon as Kallie disappeared.

"You researched her?" Jerreon knew without asking.

The old man dipped his head in acceptance. "I was concerned. You will find many people here are not what they portray. Do not get me wrong, there are many good and honest people, but there are those who aren't. Money and power is hard on even good people."

"As you can tell by Lysias, we still have such problems rise up occasionally." Jerreon walked to the case that held the coins he'd sold. "But I am pleased you like Kallie. I wish to ask another favor, one above any you have done for me already."

He looked back at the man. "If in dealing with Lysias, it does not go as I plan, I would like you to see to Kallie. Make sure she is taken care of. Protected. I know I ask a great deal, especially if Lysias were to survive and I were not."

Adam held up his hand stopping him. "You need not say more. I will see she is safe and provided for."

"Thank you. There is one more item which I would ask of you. How do I go about marrying Kallie, legally to your people?"

"When would you like this to happen?"

"As soon as possible. She is leaving the day after tomorrow. I would prefer her to leave as mine."

"I will see what we can do. We should have your ID sometime tonight. That will help."

"Thank you."

110

The man looked past him. Jerreon didn't need to turn to know Kallie stepped into the room. He also knew she was anxious but nothing was wrong. He went to her and took her hand, bringing it to his lips. "Be at ease. I will be right back. I'm just going to clean up so we can eat."

He leaned down to give her a quick kiss and was tempted to deepen it. She loved him. It came to him in her every touch.

It took effort to release her and step into the hall.

Chapter Nine

"You love him." There was no question in Adam's words.

Kallie wanted to follow Jerreon but turned to Adam. She didn't attempt to deny it. "Yes. I know the time has been too short."

"But it doesn't matter," Adam said sagely.

This time she shook her head.

"If it is right, it shouldn't. Nothing should." He walked to her and took both her hands in his, similar to the way Jerreon did, but all his touch held for her was compassion and support. "You worry about him?"

"Did he tell you where he's from?" She bit her lip.

"Not the actual place, but he's given me enough ... clues to know he's not from this planet."

"And you believe it?" She searched his face for doubt and didn't see any.

"Do you?" he asked in way of answer.

"Yes."

He squeezed her hands, then released one to slide his arm around her back, turning her toward the door. He drew her out on the balcony. They walked together slowly to the stone wall above the cliff. "Our Jerreon is a most unusual man, and not because of where he's from. Something tells me he was a great man there. He has given up everything to do a duty that probably he is the only one who could. He will need help and support. Together we can give him that, but you are the only one that can give him the other thing he'll need here – love. And after he has completed his quest – a purpose."

He gazed out over the water. "At first, after figuring out a few things about him, I was concerned about you. I am not now. You are a match for him. I'm an old man and a rich one. But it has not always been so. I grew up in humble circumstances, the son of a farmer. I worked hard and was smart, but mainly I was a good judge of character. Now, though, I choose to no longer apply myself to the business world other than to manage my assets, but I'm still a good judge of character. You, I perceive are of good character, so I will give you some advice. I would give my entire fortune for just one more day with my wife and child. They were taken from me thirty-four years ago. An accident while taking my son to school, on a day that I was too busy to stop long enough to say I loved them. We never know how long we get with the one we love. Cherish each day."

"I will." Kallie brushed back a tear that slipped down her cheek. "Thank you." She hugged him.

"I thank you, also." Jerreon stepped up and wrapped his arms around them both.

After a moment, Adam spoke again. "Well, we better sit down and eat. My chef will not be happy with me if we ruin the fine meal she made by our dallying."

As soon as they settled at the table, the food was served, and conversation turned to a much more relaxed and happier topic. Kallie told them about her writing, then they moved on to compare childhoods.

Finally, Kallie couldn't help asking the obvious question that had been avoided. "Where are you from exactly?"

Jerreon looked at them both as if assessing them for their reactions. "The place I came from is called Lantis. I grew up just outside the city. My planet is hundreds of light-years away. My galaxy is just a speck to yours."

"Then how did you get here?" Kallie leaned forward.

"We call it a Syndais. It is a link between planets. It connects and uses close to what you refer to as a wormhole in space."

"So, after you get Lysias you will go back through?"

He felt pain flare up in Kallie and reached over the table for her hand. "No! Even if it were possible, I would not leave you."

"Why is it not possible?" Adam asked. "Your people have obviously been here before and returned to your world."

"After I went through, the link had to be closed because it was unstable. We use crystals to help stabilize the Syndais. Lysias tried to take the crystal with him."

"But it broke." Kallie reached up to finger the shard that hung around her neck, remembering what he'd told her.

"Yes. Without a stabilizer the link cannot be left open long. It causes an imbalance that can be detrimental to both worlds."

"You mentioned something about that." Kallie thought back.

"Yes. We at one time developed … a base here to study your people. You were interesting because you were so similar to us, though quite behind in advancement. My people foolishly remained too long. The Syndais started to fail. It caused earthquakes and floods before the base could be brought home. It is recorded many people died. And there was so much destruction here, and on our planet. It was a time of sorrow. There never has been allowed such an endeavor again."

"Atlantis." She exchanged looks with Adam, who nodded.

"How is it you know of this?" Jerreon looked between them.

"To us it is a lost, fabled city. People have been looking for it for centuries," Kallie answered him.

"It was called after our capital city." Jerreon confirmed. "Over the centuries teams have come through to observe and study, but none are allowed to stay for any length of time. That is how we gained the crystal. The cave it came from is here, on this land, but some ways away. The crystals resonate with the energy of the Earth and my people. It drew my people to it. I plan to visit the cave. I figured Lysias would head there as soon as he recovered the other piece of the one he has. But now that he knows I am here he will wish to deal with me first."

A shiver ran through Kallie.

Jerreon reached over and laid his hand on hers, squeezing lightly.

"Why don't you two take a walk and watch the sunset. I'll be in the study when you're ready to say goodnight." Adam stood, leaned down, and to Kallie's surprised kissed her on the cheek.

She watched the old man go, feeling oddly warm toward him. "I like him." She turned back to Jerreon.

"Yes." Jerreon said, stepping around her to hold her chair for her in a show of what she thought of as old-world manners. *Maybe older than she thought.* "It is sad that he lost his family."

"He has a new one now. Though we cannot replace his real one, we can ease his loss." He took her hand again, interlocking their fingers. Together, they strolled through the gardens. "Does it bother you? Where I am from?" he asked.

"It seems unreal in a way to me." She stopped and turned in front of him, looking up. "When I look at you all I see is you. What I feel is love."

He brushed his hand over her cheek and dipped his head to kiss her. "I am just a man." He kissed her again. "A man who had to come a long way to find love." When he kissed her a third time, he pulled her tight to him as Kallie slid her arms around his neck.

They broke the kiss and he wrapped his arm around her, keeping her to his side as they walked on, stopping over the rocky point to watch the sunset. Kallie sighed, leaning back against his chest. The sun dipped into the ocean and disappeared leaving behind wisps of pinks and oranges tinting the sky.

She yawned, feeling oddly content.

"You are tired, My One." He nuzzled her neck.

"It has been a busy couple of days."

"With many emotional shifts," he added for her.

"Yes." She agreed, snuggling deeper against him.

"I think it would be good if I returned you to your place of sleep. What would you like to do tomorrow?"

"Spend it with you."

She felt him shake with a light laugh. "That is a given. But the next day you are to leave, did you want to go see your ship that is a museum? I think that would be interesting to see. I will come get you. We can eat breakfast, then go."

"Okay." She turned in his arms, arching to initiate their next kiss, which continued until they were both breathing hard.

Silently, he led her back to the study where Adam sat at his large carved desk.

"In, so soon?" Adam looked up.

"I would take her to her room now."

He picked up the phone on his desk. "They're ready to leave now," he said into it and put the receiver down.

"Before you go." He held something out to Jerreon.

Kallie looked to see what it was.

"An international driver's license and passport. We put you from England. I thought it might cover some of your speech. Also here is a cell phone. I already put in my personal number, as well as Edward's, Sam's, the head of security here and the house phone. And, of course, Kallie's number." He glanced at her for reaction, a glint in his eyes.

She just tipped her head and smiled. If he was able to produce a passport, she wasn't going to question his ability to get her phone number. He probably even had her dental records.

"Thank you. I will see Kallie home then be back. If that is still acceptable?"

"Yes. In fact, if you want to get her belongings and return, I can have a room prepared. You are most welcome here."

"Thank you, but I'll be fine there for the night."

"If you are sure, I'll see you tomorrow." He stood to come around the desk and walk them out. At the top of the steps, he kissed her cheek.

"I swear I have been kissed on the cheek more today than I have in my whole life. You have to love men with old world charms."

Adam laughed. "Why don't you add my number to your phone, in case you need anything?"

"I will. Thank you for everything. Goodnight."

"Goodnight, dear."

Kallie settled back into the seat. "I feel like a princess." She stretched her legs out in front of her.

"This is nice, but I would like to drive a car. Adam said he would see to it." Jerreon followed her motion of stretching out his long legs as he wrapped an arm around her.

"Do you have cars?"

"We have something similar. It does not have wheels. It goes over air."

"A hovercraft?"

He touched the device on his wrist then nodded. "Yes, that would be a close approximation."

He described his home to her until they arrived back at the resort. He walked her to her door. "I would linger, but then I would not want to go. So, I will say farewell."

"Goodnight."

He stared down at her a moment before swooping in to kiss her, hard and thorough, before he released her and strode away, leaving Kallie to still her racing heart.

She wondered what he would say if he knew she'd never been kissed like that before.

"I know." The words hit her clearly along with a wave of satisfaction. *"Sleep well, My One."*

ॐ

Jerreon sat in the passenger seat next to Sam Faulkner, Adam's head of security and listened as the man covered every aspect of the car, and how to handle high performance driving. It had taken him all of ten minutes to 'get the hang of it', as Sam referred to it. Satisfied, Sam moved on to instructing him in some advanced evasive driving techniques, as Adam suggested. Sam finished the explanation then took them through the course once then turned the car over to Jerreon. He followed the man's every move, liking the response and power of the vehicle.

"Why don't you take it around a couple more times and then we'll be done," Sam said.

"Yes. I would like to go see Kallie."

"Would you like to take the car? Adam approved it if I felt you were ready, and I think you are."

Jerreon thought for a second, wanting to show her what he'd accomplished, but shook his head. "I think not. It would be better if I learned my way around first."

"You know how to use the nav."

"Yes, but I would not want to endanger Kallie."

ॐ

Two hours later, after picking up Kallie and eating breakfast together, they stood waiting to buy tickets to go onto the aircraft carrier the USS Midway. He was content to follow her anywhere she wanted to go. The parks with the land or sea animals sounded most interesting, but he decided he would prefer to have more time for them, so they elected to save them for a later date.

He hadn't told her yet, but Adam was trying to arrange everything for their marriage to take place that evening. Adam promised to call when all was set, then he would let her know. He hoped she wouldn't be disappointed about not having her family there, but he wanted them married before she left the next day.

There was much love in her voice when she showed him pictures of her family and talked of them. During breakfast he'd broached the subject, actually she had, commenting about her calling him, Her One. He had felt her pleasure in it.

"You know, you use that term as wife," she'd said.

He knew she was after his thoughts. He'd been more than happy to give them to her.

"Here, for me to you, it would be wife." He'd restated. "For you to me, it would be husband. Though, it still must be made so, but as you have said, it is acceptable."

She nodded. "What are you thinking?" She looked up to him and touched his cheek. She'd made the motion several times that morning.

"Open your mind to me and see," he challenged her.

She took a deep breath and reached to touch the crystal.

He felt the stirrings. "That's it, concentrate on me. Only me."

Her touch was soft and slightly shaky. He stretched out with his mind to strengthen the link.

"You're thinking of marrying me," she whispered.

"The sooner the better," he said into her mind. "Will this be a problem without your family?" He searched for her reaction. All he found was love and certainty.

"No, all I want is to be with you."

"It is all I want, also."

"Freeze! You, big man, put your hands up." A voice demanded harshly.

Jerreon turned ready for an attack, shoving Kallie behind him, their link dissolving but not before he caught a flash of fear.

"Freeze!" The word was repeated.

Two men wearing uniforms stood about six meters away. Their hands extended out toward him, holding, what he figured, was some kind of weapon.

"Jerreon, don't move," Kallie said.

"What is this?" he asked.

"Put your hands up," a younger, dark skinned man ordered.

"Jerreon, slowly raise your hands above your head," Kallie said gently, but he still heard fear. "They are law enforcement officers."

"But why are they talking to me?" He studied the men who eyed him apprehensively. The younger scowled up at him.

People around them pulled back and stared as if he were some kind of beast or demon.

Kallie touched his arm. "I'm not sure but just do as they say until we can figure out what's happening."

"Move back please." The other officer, older than the first, motioned to her.

Kallie stayed her ground. "May I ask what this is about?"

"Kallie, move back." Jerreon got the perceived danger now, as alarm filled the crowd. He wanted to shift away from her, but was afraid to make any movement for fear the men might react and harm her by mistake. The younger man was getting more agitated, though he was trying to hide it behind his bluster. Jerreon slowly raised his hands, and to his relief Kallie took a couple steps away.

"What's going on?" she repeated her question.

"There is a warrant out for his arrest," the older man said.

"What? That's impossible. For what?" she objected.

"Ma'am, please stay back and be still. We don't want any trouble with you." The younger man glanced nervously in her direction. Kallie moved back and, to Jerreon's relief, shifted the man's focus back on him, but it didn't stay, flicking around.

"Kneel down," the older man instructed, more calmly. "Cross your ankles and place your hands behind your head."

Jerreon started to comply. A shriek split the air follow by the wail of a child. Out of the corner of his eye, Jerreon saw a flailing child push back from the woman holding him and tumble over the dock.

The woman screamed.

"Freeze." The younger officer yelled and fired.

A projectile burst from the weapon. Jerreon locked his mind on it to assess the danger. He started to step out of the way, then realized its path would pass him to Kallie. He spun, placing himself directly in front of her.

Chapter Ten

Energy hit Jerreon. Pain flicked across his senses a moment before he could clamp down on it. Swiping the projectiles from his chest, he willed the energy through his body, pooling it in his hands. He thrust his hands straight up, palms out and forced the energy out into the sky where it crackled and fizzed out.

His ears rang with the continued screams from the mother as he turned and jumped. Jerreon cleared the post of the railing, flattening his arms to his sides, and brought his feet together. He arrowed into the water. Tendrils of energy still ricocheted through his body hampering him a second before he locked on the child.

Jerreon folded over then pulled his arms through the water propelling himself down. It took eight strokes to reach the boy. Snagging an arm around the small, limp figure, he started up. He broke the surface lifting the boy high out of the water.

"Over here." One of the people looking down motioned him to the side, and he saw a ladder leading into the water. It only took a couple strokes to reach the bottom rung.

He hoisted the child onto his shoulder and started to climb. Half way up he heard the boy cough. A cry escaped the child as they reached the top.

Jerreon handed the boy over to a man reaching out for him, and climbed the last rungs until he stepped off on the dock. Kallie reached him, throwing her arms around him in much the same manner the crying woman did to her son.

"I am wet," Jerreon said, trying to ease her back, not that his efforts had any success.

"Are you all right?" She ran her hands from his shoulders down his arms to his hands turning them up to check them. Her gaze and hands came back to his body. He flinched when she touched where one of the points had hit him. She stilled, and her hands went to his shirt. He caught her hand before she could pull it up.

"I am well." He cupped her face, forcing her to look up at him. He kissed her forehead trying to hold his sodden body back from her. "The child?" He looked back to see the crying boy held tight to his mother. He appeared to be fine but frightened.

"Freeze!" The word came again.

"What?" Kallie spun, placing herself in front of him.

"He is still under arrest." The older officer stood facing them. He didn't seem as belligerent as before, but he was serious, duty minded.

"Kallie." Jerreon placed a hand on her shoulder.

"What am I to do?" He looked at the man.

The officer seemed taken back by the question. "Turn and put your hands behind your neck.

Jerreon moved Kallie to the side and complied. The man came forward, took hold of his wrist and brought it down snapping a binder on it. He did the same to the other wrist and then turned Jerreon to face him.

"There is a paramedic unit on the way to check out you and the boy." The man looked him up and down. "Though you don't seem to need it. How'd you take that jolt and not go down."

"I do not understand."

Before the officer could answer, the woman with the child came up. "Thank you." Tears still streaked down her face. "Thank you so much. He got scared when I freaked at what was happening. I've never seen an arrest before." She glanced at the officer then looked back to Jerreon. "I don't know what you did but thank you."

"You are most welcome." Jerreon dipped his head then smiled to the boy who stared at him in awe.

"He didn't do anything," Kallie said in his defense. "We don't know what this is about." She looked at the officer.

"I'm sorry, ma'am, but we have to take him in." He appeared quite apologetic.

The medic arrived and headed toward him when Officer Osborn said he'd been 'tased'.

"I am all right," Jerreon said when the medic approached him. "See to the child."

"My partner will."

A minute later, the medic shrugged and looked to the officer. "He appears fine, if anything his pulse is a touch low for what happened. You sure he got hit with the Taser?"

"Oh yeah. We saw the energy come out of his hands like bolts of lightning. Never seen it do that before." Officer Osborn stayed close while his partner kept everyone else back.

The paramedic shrugged again. "No sign. He's fine. You can take him."

"May I come?" Kallie asked.

The officer hesitated. "It would be better if you followed in your own car. I can give you directions."

"We were dropped off. I have no way to follow."

The officer debated, then glanced at the boy and nodded. "Normally it's not allowed."

"Thank you." Kallie jumped on the acceptance.

"You have to ride in back," he said it as a warning.

"That's fine." She followed them to the car. Jerreon ducked low. It was hard for him to get in with his hands behind his back.

"I'll call Adam when I find out where they're taking us."

"Maybe you should remain here."

She was shaking her head before he finished the sentence, though he knew she hadn't read his thoughts. "I'm staying as close to you as I can."

The two police officers got into the car. "Can you tell us what's happening?"

"You don't know?" The younger man said incredulously.

"No." Kallie again scowled at him.

"Your boyfriend took out a border crossing last night."

"What?" Kallie expressed the shock he felt.

"There's no denying. They got it all on video." The younger man said, then quieted when the older man cleared his throat.

Jerreon wasn't sure what this video was but his mind already came up with an unpleasant conclusion – it had been Lysias, which meant he could be in the city. Closer to Kallie than he wanted him.

"You will stay close to me, My One," he said softly.

"Hey, no whispering," the younger officer snapped. "Or she's out right here."

"It is not safe for her. She needs protection." He leaned close to the clear screen that separated them.

The two men exchanged looks.

"She'll be safe where were going," the older answered.

Jerreon settled back the best he could. Kallie leaned into his shoulder.

A few minutes later they were led into a large building and up a lift, where he was taken into a room with a glass panel on one side. His arms were released from the bindings, brought around in front of him, then the bindings put back on.

To his relief, Kallie was settled at one of the desks in the larger room outside the glass where he could see her.

The first thing she did was pull out her phone, undoubtedly to call Adam. Jerreon didn't mind the room, but wished he'd been wearing clothes from his home. His new ones held the water, and were uncomfortable to remain in now they were wet.

Kallie barely hung up when four people got off the lift. A woman, a tall black man and two other men. They went to the officers who had brought him there and their supervisor. He didn't need to try to reach out with his mind to know they were talking about him. Especially as every once in a while they'd look his direction.

Finally the group split up. One man went to talk to Kallie, another and the supervisor disappeared from view while the other man and woman entered the room he was being held in.

"Mr. Ander. I'm Agent Truman," the woman said. "This is Agent Rigby. We are from Home Land Security and have some questions for you. Can you tell me your activities of last night?"

"I had an evening meal with Kallie −"

"Kallie is Miss Martin?" the man interrupted.

"Yes, she is my ..." he had to search to the term, "fiancée. We were with a friend, Adam Bacchus, at his house. After I took Kallie back to where she is staying, I then returned to Adam's. That is where I am staying."

"You're not staying with Miss Martin?" Agent Truman asked.

"We are not married yet." His answer seemed to take both the woman and man by surprise.

"And when was this."

"I am not quite certain of the time. I have not got used to it yet. We watched the sunset. Kallie might be able to tell you. Or Adam, or Edward."

"Who is Edward?" Rigby asked.

"He is the young man who is Adam's driver."

"Driver?"

"Yes, he drove the car there and back."

The two exchanged looks.

Jerreon decided to reach out to see what they were thinking.

First, he focused in on the woman. *"Who is this guy?"* The words ran through her mind.

The man's thoughts were more odd. *"Driver, limo. So, what was he doing breaking up the border?"*

"I did not break your border," Jerreon said.

The man glared at him while Agent Truman cleared her throat.

"Oh, we have a pretty good photo of you doing it." She opened a folder she carried and dropped a picture on the table in front of him.

Jerreon leaned forward to look at the grainy photo of Lysias. There were two men on the ground and a section of the barrier ripped aside.

"I don't think we have many men in the area that are well over six and a half feet tall, in their thirties, with hair so blond it appears almost white. Just not that common," the woman said. "You want to try again."

"The man is Lysias Ptolemaios." Jerreon met her gaze then looked to the man.

"Who's that? Your evil twin." Skepticism rang in Rigby's voice.

"He is evil, but we are not related."

Before he could say more there was a knock on the door and the black man opened it and stuck his head in the room. "Ander's lawyers are here."

Frustration showed on the pair. They followed the other man out. Jerreon looked out the window to see Kallie standing with Adam and two other men dressed in suits.

CB80

Kallie was getting frustrated. She'd been trying to convince them that it couldn't be Jerreon, but they wouldn't listen to her.

"You really ought to think about changing that story because you are pressing close to being charged as an accessory," Agent Johnson threatened her.

"I am telling you the truth. Jerreon and I had dinner with a friend. His name is Adam Bacchus. If you'll ask him, I'm sure he'll confirm it."

"Then maybe you would explain this." He held up a tablet.

As she watched, a video began to play. Dread hit her. A man who, from the distance of the camera, looked a lot like Jerreon walked into view. A guard came out to him. Before the guard had a chance to react, Lysias thrust out his arm and struck him in the chest, knocking him back against the building. The man dropped limply to the ground. Two more guards rushed him. Then without warning, they jerked and flew aside as if they had been tossed away like a small pest of little consequence.

Lysias turned toward a truck and the engine blew up. The man in it barely scrambled out before it was engulfed in flames. Two guards opened fire with their guns. Lysias flinched as if one bullet might have hit him, but he didn't stop. He slashed his hand out in front of him and the others bullets seemed to go wide. With another jerky movement from Lysias, the guards' guns were ripped from their hands, and the men thrown back.

There was a flash and the screen blacked out for a moment. When the screen came back up, Lysias was nowhere to be seen. All that was left was destruction.

"Do you want to try again?" the man asked.

"It is not Jerreon." Kallie flinched and swallowed hard, not as much from what the agent said or Lysias did, as the thought that Jerreon was to face him. There was no doubt Lysias was powerful, and Jerreon said he was vicious but, for some reason, she hadn't expected this. Even after her encounter with him.

She wondered what abilities Jerreon had. Surely to be sent after Lysias, he must be equal to the challenge.

"Are you going to tell me again that is not the same man?" The agent waved his arm to the interrogation room where Jerreon waited.

"Yes. That is not Jerreon. That man's name is Lysias." She hoped Jerreon wouldn't mind her telling. Though she couldn't say what difference giving his name would make.

"Lysias," the man repeated. "Lysias what?"

"I don't know. Tole something, I think. Jerreon told me, but I don't remember."

"So Ander knows him?" Johnson pressed.

Kallie didn't know how she should answer that. She really couldn't say Jerreon was sent here to get him, especially when she figured 'get him' meant in the permanent way. "They are enemies."

Johnson leaned back against the desk and crossed his arms over his chest. His eyes bore down on her.

To the side of the room the elevator chimed and the door opened. Adam stepped out with Edward by his side and two other men in suits.

Kallie wanted to cry in relief. The man followed her gaze and stood to meet Adam as he approached.

"Agent Johnson, Home Land Security." He stuck out his hand.

"Adam Bacchus." Adam shook his hand. "My driver, Edward James, and Hawthorne and Jones, two of my attorneys. I believe you have a friend of mine here." Adam then looked past him. "Are you all right dear?"

"Yes. I've tried to tell them they have the wrong man, but they don't believe me."

"It will be all right." Adam turned back to the agent who joined the other. "No matter what you think you see from your video, I can assure you, you have the wrong man. Jerreon Ander was with me or in the presents of my driver all evening."

He nodded to Edward. "We had a late dinner at my house, which several of my staff can also testify to. After dinner, Jerreon saw Kallie back to her hotel. Edward drove him, then he brought him back to my house, where we talked until after midnight. This is the video log from the estate. The time is recorded on it." He handed them a disk. "Also, this is the access on the GPS for the limo. It can verify they were nowhere near the border and had returned before the incident at the border happened."

One of the attorneys stepped forward to take over for Adam. "You can verify the information, but I would suggest you release Mr. Ander first."

Ignoring him, one of the agents took the disk and put it into the computer, opening the file. Skimming over the images, Kallie saw them at dinner, then her and Jerreon walking out in the garden. There was a shot of them getting into the limo, and Jerreon returning with a time stamp that put him at about forty minutes later.

The agent nodded to another, who went in and returned with Jerreon, who was rubbing his wrist. Kallie sprang out of the chair, reaching for him.

"I am still wet," he said, but wrapped his arm around her.

"What happened to you?" The corner of Adam's lip curved up in the first hint of a smile since he stepped from the elevator.

"I took a swim."

Kallie shook her head. "A little boy fell in the bay and Jerreon dove in after him. I'm sorry I didn't take time to tell you, I was worried."

"Think nothing of it. I just should have brought you some clothes, though it looks like you are almost dry."

"If you don't mind, we'd like to ask Mr. Ander some questions," Agent Washington spoke up. "Miss Martin said that you knew the man in the video. That his name is Lysias."

Kallie wanted to groan and say she was sorry. *"It is all right."* The words came to her.

"Yes. I told the others that also." Jerreon tightened his hold on her.

"Can you give us his last name?"

"Ptolemaios. But it will not help you. He will not be found in any of your information systems."

"How do you know this man?"

"We are from the same place. Ptolemaios is a criminal, a cunning, dangerous man. If any of your people encounter him, they should use extreme caution. He will not hesitate to kill."

The people around the circle exchanged looks.

"You say that as a certainty," Agent Truman said.

"It is. He will eliminate anyone he perceives as a threat," Jerreon answered straight out, causing the agents to exchange looks again.

"One of the officers told us you said Miss Martin was in danger. Is that correct?" Agent Rigby asked.

"I did not want her to be left alone. Lysias will come after her."

That got shocked responses from those around them.

"Do we need to take her into protective custody," Washington asked.

"If Lysias Ptolemaios comes after her you cannot protect her. She must remain with me."

"We'll be moving her to my estate, where my security can watch over her." Adam added to shift how Jerreon's statement sounded.

Though Kallie figured the agents weren't fooled.

"I would remind you not to take the law in your own hands." Agent Rigby's comment proved it.

"It is not my desire to infringe on your laws."

"Now," Adam interrupted. "If there isn't anything else? We have a special appointment to attend." He turned and started toward the elevator, not giving them an opportunity to protest.

One of the lawyers handed over a card. "If you have any other questions." He let it hang with that. "Do you have all your belongings?" he directed the comment to Jerreon.

"I have them." Kallie said.

The lawyer motioned for her to go in front of him. Jerreon went with her and Adam to the elevator.

"Well, that was eventful." Adam grinned once the elevator doors closed. "I've never had to go get someone out of jail before. Interesting experience."

Kallie leaned over and gave him a kiss on the cheek. "Thank you. I didn't know what else to do."

The elevator opened and they got out. Adam placed her hand on his arm, while Jerreon took her other arm.

"You did just fine." He patted her hand. "I think it best not to leave him in government hands too long. Besides, we can't very well have the groom in jail and miss his wedding, can we?"

"Wedding?"

"He's been having me work on the details. I finally had everything all arranged when you called. We do need to stop so you can get your license, but we can take care of that on the way home."

Kallie looked from him to Jerreon.

"I was going to ask you when I found out if it could be done. Is this acceptable to you?"

For the first time, Kallie noticed what seemed to be apprehension in Jerreon. As if he was afraid she would actually deny him. Certainty filled her along with love. "Yes, it is very acceptable."

CR80

Kallie looked at herself in the full-length mirror, watching the woman doing her hair set in the last jeweled comb. Her long hair was piled on her head then cascaded down her back. It looked perfect with the flowing white

132

gown she wore that was wrapped at her waist with a gold cord. She looked like a Greek goddess.

She had no idea how Adam found the dress, but it was amazing, fitting for some reason. She wondered what Atlantians actually wore for weddings. She hoped Jerreon liked this. Kallie couldn't believe she was marrying him with the setting sun. Glancing to the window, the sun was getting lower. Adam would come get her soon. Was Jerreon already waiting on the patio?

When they returned from the police station, after getting the license then swinging by to retrieve her belongings, they were whisked into separate rooms to prepare. A woman had arrived with her dress while she was in the bath, followed by the woman from a spa who pampered her until it was time for her to dress and have her hair done.

Kallie had never been so indulged in her life, but the thought of marrying Jerreon was what really thrilled her.

There was a knock at the door.

"Yes," she answered.

The door opened and Adam stepped in wearing a light gray suit with an aqua colored tie and handkerchief in his pocket. He stopped and stared at her. "Gorgeous. I hope this is acceptable. I know it is customary for the bride to pick her own, but—" He broke off.

"It's beautiful. And I think quite fitting. You have gone to a lot of work to make this special. Thank you."

"It was my pleasure. And I just contacted the right people." He stepped forward and held out his hand. "Ready?"

"Yes." She took his hand, moving to his side as he placed her hand on his arm.

Eve, the woman who had been doing her hair, picked up a bouquet of cascading white tiny orchids and handed it to her.

"Thank you." Kallie said to the woman before letting Adam lead her from the room. A photographer started to take pictures as they reached the top of the stairs.

Her dress flowed out behind her as they descended down the marble stairs. The double French doors out to the patio were open. As they reached the bottom, she turned and her gaze landed on Jerreon. He was devastatingly handsome in a suit about the same color of Adam's. His eyes met hers and she saw nothing else as she crossed the floor.

At the doorway Adam stopped, taking her hand off his arm. Kallie glanced to him then froze as he placed her hand on her father's arm.

"It is only proper." Adam smiled. "At least I got to take you this far."

Kallie's brought her hand up to cover her mouth and had to blink rapidly to hold back tears. She glanced back to Jerreon. Her mother and brother with his wife and their two children stood not far from him.

She looked back at the man who gave her the most amazing gift. "Adam," was all she was able to get out. Kallie stepped in to kiss his cheeks. He hugged then released her, going to take his place next to Jerreon.

"I can't believe you're here." She turned back to her father, who stood just a couple inches taller than her with hair whiter than Jerreon's, but his from age.

"Mr. Bacchus sent a plane for us. I couldn't believe it when he first called, especially since we hadn't heard from you." His reprimand was gentle. "We were extremely concerned. I felt a little better after meeting Jerreon, but the look on your face when you saw him said it all." He kissed her forehead as he had since she was a little girl. "You love him and that makes it okay."

"I do love him, and I'm so glad you're here."

Music started to play from a three-piece chamber orchestra set off to the side.

"I think that is our cue. Your man seems to be getting a little anxious."

Kallie got lost again in Jerreon's gaze the moment she looked at him. Love flowed from him. She tried to send her love and thanks. He reached out taking her hand as she approached, his gaze skimming over her. *"You are so aptly named."* He brushed his lips over hers.

"You're supposed to wait until after the ceremony," Adam whispered beside him.

Jerreon smiled and turned to the man standing next to the railing, who was a judge and friend of Adam's.

The judge started to speak, but Kallie lost the words looking up at Jerreon. As far as she was concerned, they'd married with their declaration on the beach, as Jerreon said was the way in his land. When she heard Jerreon repeat the words the back to the judge, her heart soared with love.

"With these rings."

Kallie almost panicked as she realized she didn't have a ring for him, but again Adam held out his hand. Two bands lay in his palm, the smaller crowned with a large sapphire or blue diamond, she didn't know which, but it was the color of the crystal around her neck. When Jerreon picked up the band for him, she caught the flash of a smaller, identical colored stones spaced around the band.

"You like?"

"Oh, yes."

She felt a wave of approval.

"You may now kiss the bride."

Jerreon didn't seem to need any prompting. He cupped her face in his hands and eased her to him to meet his lips. *"My One,"* the words floated through her mind, a declaration of joy and promise.

Kallie kissed him, giving herself over to love.

"Oh my." Her mom's gasp penetrated her mind.

Kallie pulled back, blushing as she turned to her family.

"Oh my," her mother said again, rushing up to wrap her arms around her. "This was such a surprise. You look so beautiful."

"Yeah, sis. Who knew?" Dillon, her brother, crowded in.

"She's a princess," Aubrey, her niece declared.

Everyone laughed.

"Have you met Jerreon?" She reached for Jerreon's hand, drawing him into the circle.

"When we arrived, he and Mr. Bacchus greeted us." Dillon said.

"Adam, we are family now." Adam clapped Jerreon on the back.

After a few minutes, they moved to where the table was set waiting for dinner to be served.

"Oh, what an amazing meal," her mother said when they finished. "Really, it's an amazing day." She looked to her daughter. "We got a call this morning from Adam that you were getting married and if we could make it, he would send a plane for us. I'm not sure if I truly believed it until that fancy plane touched down and the pilot came out to greet us."

"I can't believe you could get away on such short notice." Kallie glanced at Jerreon then back to her family.

"We wouldn't have missed this," her father said.

"And Adam said he'd have us home tomorrow," Dillon added.

"Where are you staying tonight?" She looked at her family then to Adam.

"Your room. Since its open, and you had it through tomorrow, it made sense."

"We thought," Dillon reached over and tweaked Aubrey's hair, "we'd take the kids to Sea World in the morning then we'll be taking off about seven o'clock. It's kind of nice flying on a private plane. We don't have to be there an hour and a half early for check-in. Thanks, sis. Nice little vacation."

"I'm glad to be of service."

"If you're ready, Edward will take you to the resort now," Adam gave what Kallie could say was a very subtle hint.

"True," her mother said. "It's time we get the little ones to bed. It's been a very big day for them."

Everyone around the table stood and made their way to the driveway where they exchanged hugs.

"I think I will turn in also," Adam said as the limo pulled away. "It has been quite a day. Police stations and weddings, what a combination, and of course we can't forget a swim in the bay." He grinned at Jerreon then kissed Kallie on the cheek. "Goodnight." He ambled inside whistling.

Jerreon slipped an arm around Kallie, pulling her back into him.

She sighed liking the feel.

He kissed the side of her neck. "Would you like to take a walk out to the garden before we go in?"

Kallie nodded, suddenly feeling very nervous. She was married to Jerreon. She couldn't believe it. The day truly seemed like a dream. There'd been so many emotional swings and this one she was now facing was the greatest. She didn't doubt she loved Jerreon. He'd taken up residence in every part of her heart and soul. He was everything she could have dreamed of and more. After just two days, she couldn't imagine going through life without him.

They reached the railing where their marriage had taken place and stopped. He stepped behind her and wrapped his arms around her. Below she could hear the crash of waves against the beach. Jerreon's lips brushed her neck setting off internal crashes that matched the rhythm.

"You are nervous, My One." There was no reprimand, just concern in his voice. "You are not having ... second thoughts of marrying me."

She shook her head. "You know I'm not." She leaned back into him. "I love you."

"Yes, this I know."

Kallie swallowed and looked out at the lights from ships dotting the water. "I am not very experienced in this."

"As you have never been married, I can understand that."

She almost laughed. "No, I mean I really am not experienced with men." She caught her lip between her teeth, worrying it a little.

"Kallie, all will be well."

"I know but," she looked back over her shoulder to him. "I can count the men I've kissed on one hand. And ... I've never done any more than that."

He turned her in his arms, then his hands came up to cup her face. Kallie felt his gaze caress with love. "You were not for them," he said smoothly. "Do you believe this?"

She could only nod, as what she felt overwhelmed her. He kissed her lightly, raised his head. "I love you." He kissed her again, settling in to savor. Kallie lost herself in the kiss. She felt like she was floating then realized Jerreon had lifted her into his arms.

"Would you be mine?" He lifted his head and looked down at her.

She nodded. "Yes." The word was soft but sure, and it was all he needed.

Jerreon carried her to the back stairway and up to what had been his room and was now theirs.

Chapter Eleven

Sunlight, muted by sheer white curtains, flittered into the room giving it a subtle glow. Jerreon opened his eyes and sighed in contentment, feeling Kallie snug against his body. Her hand rested lightly on his chest right over his heart. She was where he wished she could always be. He wondered when he'd get to hold her like this again. It was too soon to have her away from him, but with Lysias so close she couldn't remain here.

She was not going to be happy when he told her he was sending her off with her parents, but it was the right thing to do. He knew the truth when her brother had said they lived in a sparsely populated area. Even Lysias would have a hard time finding her there.

Jerreon placed his hand over hers, pressing it down as he kissed the crown of her head. Joy soared in him wiping away his concerns. Kallie shifted into him and made a soft purring sound. Jerreon smiled again, feeling better and better about being stuck on this world. Maybe he wasn't a man out of place, just one that had to go a long ways to find his.

Kallie's lips brushed his chest, making his heart rate jump. He looked down to find her staring up at him.

"My One." Her words reached him.

Yes, he'd definitely found his place. He pulled her up over him to say good morning in the best way he knew how.

139

CRED

They were sitting on the balcony eating breakfast when Edward came rushing up the steps. Until then, they had been left on their own. Jerreon sensed urgency blasting off the young man before Edward stopped three steps from the top.

"Adam wanted me to come," he said. "He wants you inside, out of sight. There are some government guys here."

"I thought we had Jerreon cleared of all charges." Kallie reached across the table.

Jerreon caught her hand, sending out comfort.

"That doesn't seem to be why they're here. They were asking questions about where Jerreon's from. How long Adam's known you? But I got the feeling they were asking other things."

"What do you mean?" Kallie asked. Fear glistened in her eyes when she glanced back and forth between them.

"As I left the room, I heard one of the men ask if you," he looked at Jerreon, "knew how Lysias caused the explosion and knocked the guards back without even touching them. You need to get in and stay out of sight."

Jerreon nodded in understanding.

Edward changed his focus to Kallie. "I'm sorry to disturb your morning."

"It's okay. Thanks for the warning." She watched him disappear then shifted her gaze to Jerreon. "What do we do?"

Silently, Jerreon rose with her, ushering her inside and closing the doors.

Kallie turned into him the moment the lock clicked shut. She trembled as his arms tightened on her.

"There is no reason to fear." He tilted her face up. "Adam will handle them." He tried to press his mind out to find the government men, but the distance was too far.

"Can you detect what they want?"

"They are beyond my abilities."

"I don't like this. If they're after you..." Her fear threatened to burst.

"Do not worry until we see if concern is needed." He stroked her hair.

"You don't understand what's happening."

"I do. I am an alien on your world."

A shudder ran through her and he pulled her tight.

"You know this," he said gently.

"I know, but I have all these images of old movies with aliens and the government agency hunting them down to run experiments on them."

"Shh, I do not think it will be as bad as you make it sound, though I am sure I would be of interest to your people. After all, mine have been observing yours for centuries."

"Do yours dissect mine?"

"Of course not."

"Well, I wish I could believe mine would not do that if they found you." Kallie knew he wasn't taking her worry seriously, but she was. She couldn't stop the images of him being hunted down and trapped, being strapped to a table and experimented on.

He tipped her chin up and kissed her.

She eased back, reached up to touch a lock of the white hair she'd ran her fingers through just an hour earlier. "Maybe we should dye your hair so it wouldn't be so noticeable."

"I am not sure what you mean of this?"

"We could turn it darker. Brown or even black. Light brown would probably look better on you."

"You mean change the color, like with cloth?"

The way he tilted his head at trying to understand what she was talking about broke some of the tension in her and made her smile. "I take it people don't dye their hair on your world?"

"Actually, some do. I just wanted to make you be at ease. I do not like seeing you upset. If it would make you feel better, we can dye my hair. I will let you decide."

She studied his face, running her hand through the silky strands. "I like your hair. It doesn't have to be something that would be permanent. They have stuff that will wash out in just a couple of washings." She debated it seriously. "I think it might be a good idea. At least for now, until Lysias's border crossing is out of everyone's mind."

"As you wish." He bowed his head to her.

"I might get annoyed with you if you always give in to me like that." She frowned.

"You would not like it if I always let you have your way?" He kissed her just beside her lips.

"No. I'd always worry you wouldn't be happy."

He kissed the other cheek. "I can understand this. I assure you I will not always agree. It is just in this I see merit and it is no concern to me the color of my hair, as long as you find me appealing."

"There is no worry there."

"That is good because I find you very appealing." This time his lips settled over hers. He was still kissing her when there was a knock on the door.

Kallie jerked away, spinning toward the door, putting herself between it and Jerreon as if she could shield him.

Jerreon's hands rested on her shoulder. "Relax. It is Adam. Enter," he said loudly

⋘⋙

Jerreon tried to calm Kallie, her fear was so palpable. The only problem was he really didn't know if what she feared was true. Concern radiated from Adam coming in from the other side of the door before he entered the room.

"We had visitors." Adam tried to make light of it.

Kallie ignored the attempt, going right for the purpose. "Who were they?"

"Two men, one from the government, the other military. They were interested in Jerreon. It seems Lysias caused quite a stir. I still don't think they're sure it wasn't you, but more, they really want to know if you can do the same things he can." There was a hint of question in Adams voice.

After all the help and acceptance Adam had given him, Jerreon did not feel it right to hold back the truth. "I have not tried what he did, but I imagine it is quite possible. I am sorry to have brought this trouble to you."

Adam was waving the notion away before Jerreon even finished. "I think we were meant to meet. Life was getting a bit boring for me. I was feeling old and useless. You have given me purpose. A family." Adam's gaze went to his hand on Kallie's shoulder. Jerreon picked up Adam's desire for grandchildren. The man had truly taken them to his heart as his family.

Jerreon wished there was a child on the way, but until his duty was resolved with Lysias, he did not dare allow it to happen. He should have kept himself from her for her safety, but he would not risk leaving her with his child if he failed and died.

Kallie turned, alarm sparking in her eyes. He wondered if she picked up on his thought. Again, the possibility that she had descended from his people intrigued him, or was it just that the bond between them was so complete, she'd been attuned to him or possibly both.

"There is more?" he asked, motioning Adam to the sitting area as he directed Kallie there. He settled beside her, pulling her close to him.

"Lysias cleaned out an ATM."

Kallie caught her breath obviously knowing what it was and that it was of some significance.

"An ATM?"

Adam started to explain. "It is part of a bank to get money, but you are to have an account and money in the bank to use. You are supposed to have a card like we got for you to obtain the money. Lysias had none of those things. He walked up and placed his hand on the machine and it dispensed all the money in it. Surveillance cameras on the ATM recorded the whole thing. They got some clear pictures of him. So they know it wasn't you, but still, there is enough of a resemblance." He left it hanging.

"That they are worried." Kallie finished the thought.

"Yes. Since you admitted to knowing him, and there is such a resemblance, they are targeting you."

"Where is Lysias?" Jerreon asked.

"They don't know. That's one of the things they are hoping you can help with. A police officer tried to stop him, but Lysias did something and knocked the man away. Luckily, the officer will be all right, but he doesn't remember anything about what happened."

"I do not have time to deal with their concerns." Jerreon glanced out the window, his jaw taunt.

"I think I've gotten rid of them for now."

Jerreon turned back but Kallie asked first. "How?"

"I told them you had married and were on your honeymoon. I even had your marriage certificate for proof. I'm sure they've already checked with Arthur to validate it."

Jerreon sensed Adam was enjoying his role in this more than it was a bother to him.

"What are we going to do?" Kallie's hand trembled under his.

He stroked his thumb over her knuckles, his mind made up. "First we dye my hair. Your idea has even more merits now."

Adam cocked a brow in surprise.

"Can Edward pick up what is needed to do this?" Jerreon focused on him.

"Of course, I'll send him immediately."

"A dark blond or very light brown. And make sure he gets something that will wash out after a short time," Kallie added quickly.

"You like his hair." Adam barely got the words out before Kallie answered.

"Yes." She was firm with the reply.

"Don't worry, I'll tell him. What then?" Adam turned back to him.

"We go to where Kallie's family is and spend the day with them. When they leave she will go with them."

"No." Kallie pulled back.

Jerreon reached for her, but she stood and backed away. "I would rather you not have to leave, but it is necessary," he said gently. "You will be more comfortable with your family and they will watch over you."

She backed up several more steps, shaking her head.

"I will send a couple of security guards for precaution," Adam said to him, then looked at her.

Kallie's hand was now covering her lips.

Adam stood and quietly left the room.

Jerreon rose, coming to stand in front of her. "Kallie, you knew this was to be. You were always supposed to be leaving today."

"But that was before we married. Now..." The words trembled and a tear slipped down her cheek. She looked away.

Jerreon placed his hands on either side of her shoulders, holding her still, as he eased in close.

She avoided raising her face to look at him.

He moved one hand to her chin and tilted it up.

A sob broke from her. Her eyes were bright with pools of tears as she met his gaze. Her chin trembled, fighting back the words that couldn't be held in. "I don't want to be away from you."

"I know, My One. I have no wish to be away from you, but I cannot risk Lysias getting close to you and sensing the bond between us. It would make you his target and I could not handle anything happening to you." He caressed his thumb over the smooth skin of her cheek, opening his heart to let his love flow for her to know.

"What do you think I feel? I'm afraid if we're separated, I will never see you again." A sob punctuated her words.

"I plan a very long life with you. To hold you in my arms at night and love as we did last night." He kissed her. "I have a wish to place children in you and watch them grow." He kissed her again. Tears trickled down her cheeks. He kissed them away. When her arms came up to circle his neck, he drew her tight, deepening the kisses. The next shudder that escaped her, ignited fire within him and Jerreon lifted her into his arms, carrying her back to their bed.

CஐD

Kallie glanced over at Jerreon beside her. She missed his whitish hair, but he was still devastatingly handsome as sandy blond. With his natural tan-colored skin it gave him a great California beach boy look. Until he spoke.

The expression on his face was priceless and they weren't even through the main gate of the marine park.

"Tell me again what this place is?"

"They have exhibitions of marine animals and a few others that are tied to oceans and water. It allows people an opportunity to see creatures that they most likely would never get to see in their lives. It also has a few amusement park type rides." She grinned. "You might find them interesting also. I don't know if you have anything like them on your world."

They made it through the entrance to the park.

"We'll meet my family later this afternoon at the whale show. That will give us some time on our own first." Kallie swallowed hard to keep the words from choking her. She'd lost the debate about staying with him, and she understood the reasoning. It just didn't make it any easier.

He squeezed her hand. "Which way do we go?"

She looked at the map that had been handed them when they purchased their tickets. "This way. The dolphin show is in just over an hour. We can stop and see some dolphins on the way. They're my favorite. I've always loved them. When I was a kid, I dreamed of becoming a marine biologist and working with them."

"Why didn't you?"

"One – I lived nowhere near an ocean. Two – I wasn't sure about dealing with sharks. There's something about the look in their eyes that gets me. They're kind of dark, soulless. That's it, besides their teeth."

He released her hand and slid his arm around her waist. "You'll have to show me."

"Well, we're at the right place. Look there's a dolphin." She pointed to the low pool with people gathered in groups all around it. Several dolphins swam around. As they neared, one did a flip out of the water bringing "Ohs" from the people and squeals of delight from the children. Another pulled up on its tail and looked to dance backward on the water, chattering wildly. The crowds gasped in reaction.

"Aren't they beautiful?" Kallie grabbed Jerreon's hand and darted to the edge of the tank, drawn to the mammals. She let out an excited cry like one of the children when the dolphins rose out of the water right in front of her. She reached out and reverently touched one that slid along under her hand. "Oh, you're beautiful," she cooed.

Jerreon stuck his hand out and another rose out of the water bumping his hand with its nose, then began to chatter at him with clicks and whistles.

Kallie laughed at the antics. "It's like it's talking to you."

He smiled warmly and reached out to pet another that jockeyed for his attention. "It is. Most fascinating creature."

People began to crowd around them, everyone trying to get close.

"Please." A little girl about six or seven cried out, trying to get through, but couldn't see well with all the people. Her father boosted her up but she still couldn't get close.

Jerreon looked over at the man. "May I?"

The little girl was already reaching for him. When the man nodded, Jerreon caught her under her arms and lifted her over the people between them. "Hello there. Would you like to meet them?"

"Yes." Her voice was high and cracked with desire.

Jerreon stuck his hand out over the water. Immediately, a gray head popped up. He ran his hand over it then reached for the little girl's hand, guiding it out until she touched the head. The dolphin made a clicking sound.

"She is saying hello." Jerreon told the girl.

"Hello," the girl said and then stroked it again.

"Back to your father." He lifted her over to the hands of her father.

"Thank you," the woman standing next to the man said.

Jerreon dipped his head in acknowledgement. He turned back to the dolphin as it let out another burst of clicks in animated chatter.

"She would like us to come swim with them. Is it allowed to swim in this pool?" He looked down at Kallie. "No one else is in it but several wish to be."

Kallie laughed. "No, we can't go swimming with them. That would be a fast way to get kicked out of the park. Can you really understand them?"

"I do not get the words but their intention is quite clear. You try," he urged.

Kallie hardly hesitated before pushing out with her mind. She felt a wave of pleasure and curiosity. She wasn't sure if it was the dolphins or the people flocked around.

"That is them," Jerreon answered for her. "They want to play."

A woman in a kind of uniform that consisted of shorts and a polo shirt with a logo on its pocket, squeezed in. "Please, I must remind everyone not to feed them." She glanced at them suspiciously. "They will be fed soon if you'd like to hang around and watch."

"We are just talking with them." Jerreon stroked another dolphin vying for his attention, bringing his hand around to rub under its bottom jaw.

"Where do you work with dolphins?" the woman asked as if the answer to the strange actions of the mammals dawned on her.

"I do not, but they are very intelligent and intriguing. I would like to spend more time around them." He looked down at the dolphins, concentrated, and they took off, racing through the water then executed a flip then a tail walk, in way of saying good-bye. The crowd around them applauded then dispersed, allowing him and Kallie to move away.

Kallie knew the woman was watching them, but was too happy to worry about it. She hugged Jerreon's arm, laying her head against his shoulder. She had to fight to keep from dancing. "That was one of the most incredible experiences of my life. And after the last couple days, that's saying a lot."

He intertwined their fingers. "It was wonderful. I would like to go swimming with them sometime."

"I'm afraid that can't be here, at least not today. They do have an interaction thing, but I think you have to reserve a time for it. There are places you can swim with dolphins. We'll have to check it out and go there."

"I would like that." He got a thoughtful expression. "Are all dolphins in places like this?"

"No, just a few. Most are in the oceans. Originally, they were brought into places like this to study and bring awareness. Now, the ones here are usually born in captivity. They have a large program for animals that are injured, but most are returned to the ocean once they are healed, if possible."

"I like your dolphins. I can see why you would be drawn to them."

"They have a dolphin show. That's where we're headed now. We'll see the type of things we just saw, but a whole lot more. Also, there's a killer whale show later today. That's where we'll meet up with my family." Kallie couldn't hold back the wave of sadness that passed over her at the thought of leaving him.

Jerreon leaned down and kissed the top of her head, giving her hand a squeeze.

"Killer whale?" He looked down as if to see if she was serious.

She laughed at his expression. "They are really called Orcas. I don't know the scientific name. Most people just call them killer whales. They are amazing hunters. They look a lot like dolphins but much bigger, small though compared to some whales. You've seen their pictures around everywhere here, the distinctive black and white whale. See over there." She pointed to a sign. "It's one of the park's symbols."

They stopped and went through a couple sights on the way to the dolphin show. Luckily, they were still early enough to find a space quite close to the front. They'd hardly sat down when a series of whistles reached them from behind the gate where the dolphins were waiting.

"That's the dolphins." Kallie felt her excitement rise.

"Yes, they are saying hello. They are excited to perform for us."

Which quickly became evident as the show began. The dolphins came out doing amazing leaps and flips.

"They are excited today," their trainer commented during one of his spotlights about working with the animals. "We are getting an amazing show."

It continued on until the end of the show when it was time for the dolphins to say their good-byes and go. Instead they all came over in front of Jerreon and started chattering excitedly to him.

Kallie laughed at their antics. "It looks like you really have made friends."

The trainer must've overheard her because he turned and stared at Jerreon. "It seems they found someone they want to meet in the audience. Will you please?" He motioned for Jerreon to come down.

Jerreon hesitated.

"Go on." Kallie started to laugh again. He caught her hand and stood drawing her down with him over to the trainer.

"Welcome, and what are your names?" The man extended the microphone toward them.

"I'm Kallie, and this is my husband, Jerreon." Kallie leaned forward and said in the mic.

"And what brings you here?" the man asked.

"We're on our honeymoon."

Awes and applauses erupted from the crowd.

"Congratulations," the trainer said. "Would you like to meet our crew of show offs?"

"Very much." Jerreon answered.

As soon as they walked out on the platform lip, all the dolphins came sliding up to be introduced, whistling and speaking as Kallie and Jerreon greeted each.

"Would you like to tell them good-bye?" the trainer asked.

Instead of making the hand sign, Kallie felt Jerreon think the words and followed him with her thanks and appreciation. The dolphins clicked out their farewells then wiggled back into the pool, several doing flips, while others did leaps on their way out.

The trainer stepped up to Kallie and Jerreon before they could follow the crowd out. "You must be the couple Becky was telling me about from over at the dolphin pool. She said you were both tall. We had lunch together right before the show."

"Sorry if we caused a problem."

"Not at all. We know dolphins are drawn to certain people, so she remarked upon it. I understand what she meant. That is the strongest reaction I've ever seen. Becky said you don't work with them." There was questioning in his gaze.

"No, this is the first I have ever encountered them, but I would like to spend more time with them. They are amazing. Very intelligent."

"I can agree with that. Will you let me know when you come back? I'd like to see how they react."

"It would be my honor. I would like to do the encounter you talked about in the show."

A series of shrill whistles split the air like an alarm. Jerreon froze then turned, his eyes scanning the area.

Kallie picked up the feeling the dolphins were sending out. Danger.

"Lysias is near," Jerreon said, looking back to her. "They sense him and don't like the feeling he gives off."

"Are you sure?" She didn't doubt the dolphins, just hoped they could be wrong.

"Yes. I have to go." He started to pull back.

She grabbed his arm. "Jerreon!"

He touched her cheek and gave a forced smile. "I have to try to lead him away. There are too many people to confront him here. Someone would get hurt. I cannot let him endanger others. He would kill them just to distract me." He pressed his lips to hers in a hard, swift kiss. "Your family is coming. Stay with them. I will come for you, My One." He kissed her again then broke free, striding away toward the exit.

Across the pool another volley of whistles rang out in alarm.

Chapter Twelve

"What's going on?" The trainer demanded, alarmed. "Who's dangerous? What's disturbing the dolphins? And what's this about killing."

"Can you get hold of security from here?" Kallie asked ignoring his question.

"Of course." The man nodded, eyeing her over.

"There's a very dangerous man that's wanted by the police. I'm not sure if he's in the park, but he must be close. He looks a lot like my husband, just as tall but with white hair, though he's not old. Is there any way to find out if he's inside the park boundaries?"

"We can try," he said, to her relief, taking her seriously.

He led her to where there was a walkie-talkie and called security, relaying what she said about a man wanted by the police and stressing the white hair when she repeated it to him.

Kallie didn't want Jerreon arrested again by mistake. "Tell them not to try to confront him. He's violent."

He added that then turned back to her. "Your husband is going to confront him?" he asked when she glanced again in the direction in which Jerreon disappeared.

"Only if he deems it safe with those around him."

"If this man's so violent, can your husband handle him? I know he's a big guy but −" The man let it hang.

"He's special security from where this man escaped. He's probably the only one that can." Kallie hoped that was enough to forestall any more questions, but it was her family that saved her.

Her nephew, Austin, was the first to reach her. "Aunt Kallie, Aunt Kallie. You got to meet the dolphins. We saw you, but we were way over there."

Kallie reached down to pick him up, hugging him tight, needing the contact.

Her brother reached her next. "Where'd Jerreon go?" He obviously could tell something was wrong.

Her father was right behind him and slid his arm around her.

Kallie leaned into him. "It's a long story, but there's a criminal from where he's from. Jerreon was chasing him. That's what he's doing here and how we met."

"How you met?" Her brother picked up on that. He reached out and took his son, settling him on his hip.

Her father's arm tightened even before she said the words. "The man, Lysias, attacked me and Jerreon saved me. In doing so, he lost Lysias, but he thinks he's close now, maybe in the park."

"He went after him?" There was a touch of anger in her brother's voice.

"What about your honeymoon? Is that why you're going home with us?" Her mother asked with the same attitude.

"Yes. Jerreon is afraid Lysias will come after me again. He wants me far from here until he gets him." Kallie felt tension build in her father.

"You'll stay with us then. We'll call Mr. Bacchus and see if we can fly out early," her father said.

"No." Kallie quickly halted him. "There is no need. Jerreon will see to him and if he can't find him, he'll come back here for me." She could feel the indecision in her father. "Please. Let's just enjoy ourselves and give him a chance to do his job. There's no reason to let it ruin our day."

She pressed brightness into her words to cover her need to stay. She wanted to be close. If Jerreon could get Lysias, there would be no need to send her away. But more importantly, she was afraid for him. She reached up and wrapped her fingers around the crystal, but Jerreon must have been too far away to detect him.

೧೩೪೦

Jerreon wove his way through the crowd in an easy, ground-covering lope. He scanned over people with his eyes and his mind, but didn't see Lysias until he reached the entrance. Lysias stood in the center of the parking lot as if waiting for him.

Conscious of the scattering of people, Jerreon was relieved none were coming close to Lysias's position. Jerreon took off after him in a full run, but Lysias didn't try to flee. Jerreon was only ten meters from him when a car shifted in front of his path, almost pinning him against another. Jerreon jumped the vehicle landing directly in front of Lysias so they stood facing each other.

"I should have expected you here. You still have not taken the crystal from the woman. Are you following it or the woman?" Lysias smirked, and they each started to circle around. "Why is it you haven't taken it? Does she interest you?"

Jerreon didn't comment. A large box lifted out of the back of a truck and sailed at the back of his head. Jerreon swept it away and it dropped several feet short without him even turning to look.

"They always said you were good," Lysias said. "But just how good is the question." Lysias gave him a wicked grin. "Are you going to give me some drivel about taking me back?"

Jerreon shook his head. "There is no going back. You know this."

"Yet, you came anyway, how self-sacrificing of you." He sneered. "Or maybe you realized what I did. You were always as fascinated with this planet as I was. Did you finally figure out here we can be gods?"

"You think too much of yourself."

"No!" Lysias burst, then his voice dropped low and cold. "I know my worth, and I am not afraid to reach it."

"By enslaving others?"

"That is the way it is to be. The strong survive and rule." Another car slid at Jerreon before Lysias finished talking.

Jerreon threw out his hand and it stopped. With a flick of his wrist, the car careened toward Lysias who had to jump back to miss it. Alarms went off in cars. Jerreon darted forward, closing in on the man.

An energy ball hit Jerreon, throwing him back several feet against the hood of a car. Few had the strength and talent to fight like that. Jerreon wasn't surprised Lysias could, though he hadn't shown his extent of ability before. Jerreon rolled off the car just in time to miss another bolt of energy that streaked a scorch mark up the hood of the car and melted a furrow in the window. He turned and sent back his own burst of energy.

Lysias spun away, barely missing being fried by it, but it was close enough to stagger him.

He recovered quickly. "Think about it," Lysias said forcefully. "With what we can do, no one here can stop us from anything." His voice dipped into a persuading hum.

Jerreon felt the pull. This was where the man's true talent lay − manipulation. With just his words and a push of talent, he could influence people when he chose.

"I do not think so." Jerreon pushed back with his mind bursting the bubble of numbing compliance Lysias was weaving around him. For some reason Jerreon's talent made him immune and allowed him to see Lysias for what he really was − evil.

C3ಬಿ

Kallie walked with her family, but didn't hear what they were saying or notice any of the sights. She scanned the crowd for Jerreon, hoping any moment to see him returning. She also kept an eye out for Lysias. Unconsciously, she raised her hand to the crystal pendant and her unease rose. Danger crackled in the air making her heart pound.

Kallie tried to fight down the panic that assailed her and concentrate on the otters doing their playful water acrobatics, but she could still hear whistles from the dolphins, then the air was split by another sound, sirens. They sounded at a distance coming closer, and by the volume, there were quite a few.

"Jerreon," she said aloud. "I have to go."

Her brother grabbed for her arm and missed. "I thought you were to stay with us."

She shook her head. "I have to find Jerreon. He could be in trouble."

"Kallie, he wanted you with us." Her father used his forceful voice, the one he reserved for only the most important lectures.

She knew it was true, but the need to see Jerreon tore at her. She looked out toward where the sirens blasted, then back.

"You have to trust him." Her mother's soft words won out. Still, it was the most difficult thing she'd ever done. She let her mother slip an arm around her and turn her away from where Jerreon had disappeared and the wailing ended.

C3ಬಿ

Jerreon pulled energy from the air around him and raised his palm toward Lysias. Energy shot through his hand intersecting with the ball that came from Lysias. The ball of energy impacted and burst apart. The concussion of the blast sent them both tumbling back. Jerreon hit into a car and fell to the ground. Lysias was thrown back and rolled across the ground.

Around them, cars with flashing lights on top approached as they pulled themselves up. Jerreon took a second to glance toward the police cars willing them away, but it didn't happen. He recognized the uniforms, but he didn't have time to deal with them. Though, he did experience fear for them. Lysias wouldn't hesitate to harm them.

The thought was hardly through his mind when Lysias turned and focused on the lead car. Energy shimmered around him as he pulled it in. Jerreon had little time to draw in enough energy to deflect Lysias's. His counter wasn't strong enough to burst the other apart, but it was enough to send the ball of power smashing into a light pole instead of the officers getting out of the car. The pole sheared off and toppled in a volley of sparks.

The officers instinctively ducked down behind the cars.

"Hands up!" someone yelled.

Jerreon raised his hands slowly knowing what was coming if he didn't obey. He met Lysias's gaze.

Lysias's lips pulled back in a sinister smirk.

"Stay back." Jerreon hardly got the words out when one of the cars between them and the officers started to shift toward the police. He spun and leapt. A sharp report cut the air. Jerreon felt a pain slice across his arm as he cleared the car. He landed crouched and took the impact of the car with his shoulder as he tried to draw energy up to shield him. The blow hit him hard, sliding him across the ground several feet before coming to a stop.

When he looked up, Lysias was gone.

"Freeze."

A groan of frustration built deep within him, changing to one of pain before it made its way out. He gripped his arm and looked down to see blood trickling from under his sleeve that was already soaked.

"Hands up! Drop your weapon!" One police officer ordered.

"I have no weapon," Jerreon said, easing his arms up, wincing at the sting of pain.

The thought of Lysias's favorite weapon came to his mind. He'd been surprised at Lysias's strength in pulling energy. It had to be because of the closeness they were to an energy point here on earth. That, and focusing through the piece of the crystal he carried. But Lysias's true talent was persuasion. He could make people forget they even saw him and even make some weak-willed people do what he wanted. That was why he had almost gotten away with what he did on their planet. Here on this world, with that ability, he truly could set himself up to be a god.

Jerreon pulled energy into his will. "You will let me go." He pushed out the thought with the words, letting his gaze slide over each man and woman. "You did not see me," he said slowly and started to back away as a blank look descended over their faces.

You did not see me. He repeated over in his mind. Making it behind a large vehicle, he bent down out of sight and hurried among the cars staying low.

Behind him he heard a commotion and several questions arise. "What happened?" being the prominent one.

He sprinted until he reached a group of parked buses. There he straightened and looked down to investigate his arm. He hadn't been hit with the same projectiles as the day before. This was different. It scored and tore at his flesh, and he decided it was lucky it hadn't hit him straight on. As it was, pain ripped through his system.

Jerreon groaned, pulled his pack from his shoulder and searched for the medic kit. He drew out a cloth, cleaned away the blood, then opened a pad and placed it over the wound. On contact, the pain eased and the area began to heat with a restorative warmth. Jerreon sighed and leaned back against the side of the bus.

Taking the crystal shard he carried from his pocket, he focused on it, trying to locate Lysias. There was no contact. Not even a stirring.

He'd lost him again. Frustration burned through him. He needed to figure out how to draw Lysias away from others to face him where he could challenge him without a fear of anyone being hurt.

Unfortunately, the only thing that seemed to draw Lysias was Kallie, and there was no way he was going to let him near her. His resolve to send her away strengthened. There was no doubt Lysias showed up here because of Kallie.

He didn't understand how Lysias was able to locate her. Jerreon knew he would have no problem finding her, but she was his One. Was the link between Kallie and the crystal so strong it allowed Lysias to trace her?

Jerreon shifted and groaned. He looked down at his sleeve and the blood staining his shirt. He needed Kallie. The pain in his arm had eased, and the wound was well on its way to healing, but if he walked around in a bloody shirt it was sure to bring notice.

He pulled out the replacement phone Adam had given him for the one he ruined jumping in the bay, but when he tried to activate it, nothing happened. He knew he was doing it correctly, but it was dead. He shoved it back in his pocket and forced out his mind, though he didn't really expect to reach her.

"Jerreon!" The cry that answered was a mixture of relieve and fear. *"Are you all right?"*

"I am whole. Lysias got away. Your police officers showed up."

"Have you been arrested again?" Fear eased in her voice, replaced with another type of panic.

"No, I got away. Can you bring me a shirt? I have ruined this one."

"What? Never mind. I'm on my way."

"I will meet you outside the entrance." He started to make his way that direction, swinging wide of the police. His One was amazing. He thought of being able to link with her. Few on his own world could have done it from this distance, but with Kallie it seemed to come naturally.

⋘⋙

Kallie became aware she'd stopped in the middle of the walkway with her family staring at her, while other people worked their way around the group. "I have to meet Jerreon."

"That's not −" Her mother caught her hand.

"Lysias got away." She cut her off. "Jerreon needs me to meet him. It's true." She pressed on the ending, seeing the looks of doubt.

"How?" her father asked.

"Part of a long story, but I have to go. We might catch up to you or we might be leaving. I'll call and let you know."

She turned and ran for the entrance before they could marshal any other objection. She wove her way through the people until she reached a shop just inside the entrance. Quickly, she bought the first shirt she saw that would fit him, a blue polo with a small dolphin embroidered on it that would be over his heart, and hurried out the gate.

"Over here." The words reached her the moment she cleared the exit. Kallie turned to the bus parking area. She wanted to run, but at the sight of the police cars across the parking lot, she kept her pace to a walk as she let the feel of him guide her.

Kallie fought to keep in a cry when she saw him. He leaned back against a bus looking tired and disheveled. He straightened on seeing her. She'd almost reached him when he turned enough to see the tear in his sleeve and the dark-red stain she knew was blood. Kallie dropped the bag and rushed the last couple steps.

"I'm all right." He caught her, snaking his uninjured arm around her waist and pulling her into him.

Kallie felt him take in a deep breath as if soothed by the contact with her. He held her tight a moment before easing her back to kiss her. On breaking the kiss, he tipped his head down to rest his forehead on hers and sighed. She ran her hands over his back in strokes that were to be comforting and assured herself that he was all right – except for his arm.

She pulled away. "Let me see."

"It is all right. I already tended it. It will be healed by morning."

The certainty in his statement shocked her, but when she pushed the cloth up all she could see was a bandage covering the muscle. She accepted his word.

"What happened?"

"Your police showed up."

"You were shot!" Her hands stilled as fear surged through her.

"Yes, but it was not the thing they used before." He was irritatingly calm, but his words didn't calm her.

"Is the bullet still in there?" She looked back at his arm not sure what to do.

"No, it just skimmed my arm."

"Skimmed? Maybe I better take a look." She reached for the bandage but he caught her fingers.

"There is no need. It is better it stays in place now that the healing has already started."

"Healing? That helps healing?" She studied his face hoping what she was thinking was true.

"Yes. By tomorrow it will be mostly healed and I can remove it."

"That's amazing." She eyed it again but didn't try to touch it.

"It works well except on serious wounds." He started to remove his shirt and flinched.

"Here, let me help."

Together, they eased off his shirt and stuffed it in his pack, then she helped him get the other shirt on. He touched the dolphin over his heart and smiled. She shrugged meeting his gaze. He slipped an arm around her pulling her close again, kissing her. When the kiss ended, she lowered her head back to his chest, taking in the comforting beat of his heart as his hand stroked up and down her back.

"Come, My One, let us go find your family."

He kept his arm around her as they made their way back toward the park entrance, keeping an eye on the police officers in the parking lot. They were clear of the buses and halfway to the gate when three identical, dark sedans followed each other through the parking lot heading for the police car. Kallie saw them first and pulled Jerreon behind a van in the handicap spot near the entrance.

"What is wrong?" Jerreon went on alert.

"Government guys are here, probably the same ones from yesterday." She glanced around the front of the van. "And maybe the guys from the house this morning." She shifted so she could see through the windows and watch as people got out of the cars. Three people approached the officers as the others fanned out.

Kallie felt Jerreon's hand rest on her back. "I don't think we should try for the park." She glanced back over her shoulder at him.

"Agreed. I don't want to chance them seeing and detaining you. Let's go to the car."

Kallie was so shocked at him using contractions she almost missed what he was saying. He took her hand. They made their way around the buses then ducked low, hurrying to where they'd parked at the far end of the lot.

The bright red sports car waited off by itself. So low to the ground, Kallie was still surprised Jerreon could fit in it, but it seemed perfect for him. She'd been even more surprised that morning at his confident, natural ease in handling it. The engine purred to life, deceptively quiet considering the power she knew was under the hood just waiting to be called on.

Jerreon shifted into gear and headed for the exit. Kallie kept her attention across the parking lot. No one paid them any attention as they headed out. Still Kallie didn't breathe a sigh of relief until they were clear. Jerreon moved his hand from the gear shift to rest on hers, giving it a squeeze.

"All is well," he said when she looked at him.

"I don't know if we dare go back to Adam's. They may be watching there."

He looked back at the road and was quiet a minute, then pulled over to the side, behind a row of magenta-colored bougainvillea and stopped. "You are right. They may be watching for me, but you could go."

"What? No!"

"Kallie, you know this is so. You already said this morning you knew how to drive a shift, so there should be nothing stopping you."

"A shift, yeah, but I've never driven anything like this before."

He arched his brow and she knew he wasn't buying her objection, though it was the truth. The car, Adam had blithely handed over for them to drive, was worth way more than she made in an entire year.

Jerreon smiled and cupped her face in one palm. "It is not the car that worries you. You also can see the wisdom as I can see the love behind your protest. So just say the words and kiss me."

Tears threatened Kallie as she complied, going in for the kiss. She gasped when he lifted her over the gearshift and into his lap to continue kissing her.

"I love you," he said, when the kiss ended. He brushed back her hair with a gentle caress, then kissed her again letting the heat in it grow.

"I love you," she repeated the words, dropping her head on his shoulder, her heart pounding.

"You give me pleasure." He held her tight for several minutes more. "Promise me you will go straight to Adam's. He will see you to the plane."

Kallie didn't want to agree but the need in him was so strong, she nodded. "Please be careful."

"That I will promise." He opened the door and slid out leaving her in the driver's seat.

"You're getting out here?"

"I will have you drive me just ahead, just so I know you can drive this car." His lips twitched into a smile.

"Funny. I am not going to leave you stranded. Why don't we go to the next hotel? I can get a taxi and that will leave you the car. I will go straight to Adam's," she added. "It will be just as safe as driving myself."

After a second, he nodded. "Yes."

Instead of helping her out, he closed the door and walked around getting in the passenger seat. "I know you wanted a turn."

It was enough to make Kallie smile. Adjusting the seat, she pressed in the clutch and brake, started the engine, then slipped it into gear. Letting out the clutch the car started forward smoothly.

"Oh, this is some car. I still can't believe you learned to drive it so quickly." She forced lightness into her voice. Unfortunately, it wasn't far until they came to a hotel. She pulled in behind a cab with a couple getting out.

Jerreon got out. "Are you for hire?" he asked the man while coming around to open the door for her.

"In one minute." The man eyed the performance car curiously. Then when he looked at her, he stared openly.

Kallie wasn't sure if Jerreon had noticed the man's attention and was staking his claim or what, but as she rose his arm wrapped around her, and he hauled her to him.

"Have care, My One." There was nothing subtle in the way he growled his words or the way he captured her mouth.

Kallie traced her finger down his cheek. "My One." She poured her love in the words.

His eyes brightened to a feverish point. "I will be with you when I can."

"I will be waiting."

Jerreon walked her to the car and held the door for her to slide in.

"Where will you go?" She sat on the edge of the seat, looking up.

"I will go back and see if I can pick up his trail."

Panic flared in her.

"I will use caution," he assured.

The driver returned. Kallie drew in her legs so Jerreon could close the door. Love flooded her mind as he stepped back. She pressed her fingers to the window while her other hand grasped the crystal.

"Where to?"

Kallie had to fight to look away from the man that had become her life in just a few short days. She gave Adam's address, her gaze returning to Jerreon as the cab pulled away. He stood like a sentinel – straight and tall.

"That was some ride your boyfriend has." The taxi driver started a conversation.

"My husband." Kallie could almost hear his mind changing from thinking she was having an affair to what was she doing climbing into his taxi then.

"I need to head home, but he has some business to take care of," she answered the unasked question.

"It would have to be some pretty important business to leave an Amazon goddess like that."

The words came so clearly into Kallie's mind she almost thought he'd said them aloud, until she realized she still had the crystal locked in her hand. She released the stone and settled back into the seat for the ride to Adam's.

⋐⋙

Jerreon wanted to call her back but knew he couldn't. Still he couldn't seem to take his eyes off the shrinking yellow point. He turned and strode back to the waiting sports car. Pulling back on the road, Jerreon pressed on the gas and the car shot forward in response. For a second, he let the power charge through him then eased back, not willing to risk being pulled over by a police officer for breaking a law. He needed to stay out of the attention of the authorities.

He parked away from the parking lot where they'd been earlier, got out and opened his mind, searching for Lysias. His first attempt brought nothing. Slipping his hand into his pocket, he brought out the blue fragment and tried again. He'd scanned over half the distance before he caught tendrils of power. He closed his eyes and concentrated harder. The trail solidified and he took off after it in a smooth run that covered the ground quickly.

The trail led him out to a path that ran alongside a river area and road. He followed it for several kilometers. Jerreon was almost to the point where he'd dropped Kallie off when he decided he needed the car in case it went farther. He ran back to where he parked.

It didn't take him anytime to pick up the trail again. Coming up on the hotel he'd let Kallie off at, he eased up on the gas, thinking of Kallie being there. He sensed the lingering presence of her then saw the shadow of Lysias cross over.

Dread hit hard. Lysias was hunting Kallie and he had her scent.

Chapter Thirteen

Kallie's thoughts were so wrapped on Jerreon, she was unprepared when the cab pulled up to the gate in front of Adam's estate.

"This the place?" the driver called her attention.

"Oh, yes. Sorry." She looked at the meter and pulled a couple bills out of her wallet. "Thanks." She got out, heading for the call box as the taxi pulled away. She pressed the button. The gate clicked and started to open without her having to say anything.

"Mrs. Ander."

Kallie jerked at the name, taking a second to realize it was her. She turned, only recognizing one of the two men striding toward her.

Agent Johnson reached her first. "It is Mrs. Ander now, isn't it?"

Kallie remembered Adam said he'd showed her marriage certificate to the agents that morning, not that she would deny it. "Yes." She met the man straight on, aware of the other moving around her placing himself between her and the gate. "What may I do for you, Agent Johnson?"

"Start with telling us where your husband is." There was a tightening around the man's mouth, a definite challenge in him.

"I'm not quite sure." She met his gaze.

He arched his brow. "You were just married. Yesterday I believe, after leaving the police station?" There was no missing the question in the words.

"Yes, but we were out shopping. He had a few more things to get, and I came back to pack. I'm flying out in a couple hours."

"Actually, we need you to come with us. We have some questions for you," Johnson's gaze didn't waver.

Kallie pulled back instinctively, and the other man closed in behind her.

"I'm afraid we must insist. Either we can do this the easy way or the hard way," Johnson said.

There was no mistaking that meant being cuffed.

"What's going on here?" Sam, Adam's head of security, appeared at the gate. Kallie could see Adam hurrying toward them.

"Mrs. Ander is coming in for some questioning." The other man, who until that point had remained silent, said in a gravelly voice that sounded like it once held a southern drawl before it had been raked over broken glass.

"I'll get a hold of my lawyers, Kallie." Adam's focus went right to her.

"That won't be necessary. This is a matter of national security." Johnson reached out and took her arm. "You can tell Ander to contact us though." He turned her away, not giving her any chance to object as the other man reached in his pocket and handed a card through the gate.

"So he can reach us." The man's words cut into her.

They were using her to get to Jerreon. She wanted to cry with frustration. She should have figured that. Everyone was using her against him. Kallie wished she could warn him. Wrapping her hand around the crystal brought nothing, then a feeling of foreboding hit her so strong she dropped the crystal. Dark wisps of current remained to taunt her. *"Jerreon!"* she whispered in her mind as fear for him exploded within her.

They led her across the street to a black sedan.

"Please, don't take me." She knew her plea wasn't going to work but couldn't help trying.

Johnson actually looked shocked when he turned to study her. For a moment, there seemed to be compassion in his eyes. "You're not in any danger," he said as if to be comforting.

Saying that though was as if it called up the feeling. Kallie glanced back expecting to see Lysias there, but only the other agent was visible. She didn't know his name.

"Mrs. Ander." Johnson held the car door open.

Kallie hesitated until she felt a nudge on her back forcing her forward. "You don't know what you're doing."

Johnson's brow did another lopsided arch.

A grunt sounded from the man behind her. "I think we do."

"I don't even know your name."

"Rhodes." He leveled his gaze at her.

Unable to do anything else, Kallie slid in the car. She was almost relieved when Johnson got in beside her instead of the other man. "May I at least call Mr. Bacchus to have him let my parents know I'm not going to make the plane?"

"Why don't you just call your parents?" the man probed.

"I probably can't reach them now."

Johnson nodded, but when she pulled out her phone, he tipped it so he could see the screen. Fortunately, Jerreon's number was listed under Adam's name, since she hadn't bothered switching it yet. Kallie pressed the call button. The phone went right to voice mail. Johnson took the phone and brought it to his ear.

"There's no answer." She tried to calm her pounding heart. "I'll try his other number."

Again, Johnson watched her motions.

To her relief, Adam answered before the second ring.

Johnson leaned in to listen. "Adam, they are letting me call," she said quickly. "I tried your other phone but got no answer. I was worried."

"I'll check it out," Adam answered, obviously getting her meaning that she couldn't reach Jerreon.

"Would you let my parents know I won't be coming? I don't know how long I'll be detained and don't want them to worry. Let them know I'm okay."

"Don't worry. I'll take care of it. If you can, keep me posted on what's happening."

Johnson frowned, and she was afraid he was about to take the phone from her. "I will. Thank you," she said hurriedly and hit disconnect.

Johnson's eyebrow arched up again and he held out his hand for her phone.

She handed it over. "Where are you taking me?"

"To a secure facility. It won't take long to get there. Just relax."

Kallie tried, but it was impossible as the feeling of danger grew within her. She glanced in the rearview mirror only to find the other agent staring at her so she shifted to stare out the window.

They turned the corner heading back toward the beach road. A wave of malice hit. She shuddered and twisted in the seat. Kallie saw nothing behind her but felt as if something evil was walking in her shadow. Instinct had her raising her hand to the crystal, but she stopped half-a-inch away, too afraid of what she'd feel.

"Is something wrong?" Agent Johnson turned in his seat to look out the back window.

"I don't think we're safe." Subconsciously she whispered the words.

"What did you see?" He looked at her as they pulled out onto the main thoroughfare.

"Nothing." She slipped her hand into her purse before remembering Johnson had her phone. "Please, I need my cell phone."

"Why?" the man eyed her.

"We need Jerreon." She didn't hesitate in her answer.

"Can you reach him?"

"I hope so."

To her surprise, he handed the phone over.

"What are you doing?" Rhodes asked.

"If she can bring us Ander, that's what we want," Johnson answered.

Though Kallie knew the reason, it still gave her pause, but there was no choice. She activated the phone, aware of Johnson watching her as she brought up the number again. Once more, it went right to voice mail.

"Jerreon, I think I felt Lysias. That he's after me. I don't know for sure. It's the same feeling I had from him before but stronger, and it doesn't seem to be fading. I think he's following me. I've been taken by the agents. Please call me." She cut the connection and turned in the seat again, praying to see Adam's bright red sports car racing up behind, but she didn't see it or any sign of the danger she knew was there.

೧೪೪

Jerreon pulled out the phone only to face a black screen like it had been in the parking lot. He tossed it into the passenger seat and shifted through the gears bringing power out of the precision machine. Only the need to keep Lysias in his senses kept his speed in check, though as he traveled he was sure where the man was headed.

He was close to Adam's when suddenly he lost the trail. Jerreon whipped the car to the side of the road. Wrapping his hand around the crystal, he pushed power through it.

Kallie's was the first essence that filled him. He reached for her, picking up fear, but no panic. At this point,

173

Lysias didn't have her, but he was near and she knew it. Jerreon only hoped they could get her on a plane before Lysias reached her.

Turning the car around, he followed Kallie's and Lysias's trails, headed toward the beach area. A minute later, the crystal flared and picked up a glow. When Jerreon backed off the power he was pushing, it didn't settle. He scanned the cars until his gaze landed on a silver sedan just ahead.

Lysias.

The sedan jerked into a turn and picked up speed. Jerreon thought for a moment Lysias was trying to evade him. Then the vehicle whipped around another car and arrowed in on a black sedan identical to those he'd seen in the parking lot with the government people. He didn't have to use the crystal or really even try to know Kallie was in the black vehicle. How she ended up there he didn't know and didn't have time to worry about it as Lysias closed in on the car.

Jerreon shifted, pressing down on the gas while letting up on the clutch. The car shot forward, weaving in and out of traffic. Several people blasted their horns, but Jerreon ignored them. Swerving in behind a bus, he zipped in front of a van on the other side. Jerreon shifted again, pulling in front of the bus. In a matter of seconds, Jerreon had cut the distance between them in half, but Lysias had also halved the gap between him and Kallie.

Jerreon floored the pedal.

ଔଞ

"You have to believe me. Lysias, the man you're after, is near." Kallie looked between the two men then out the back window.

"What are you, psychic or something?" Rhodes's gravelly drawl reached back to her full of skepticism.

"A month ago, or even a week, I would have said no, but for some reason, I can sense him. He freaks me out. I can feel his evil. Just as I can your disbelief," she said, daring him to challenge her statement. "You need to get help. Call your people at the parking lot and get them here. We're not going to make it to where you're taking me." That got at least a jerk reaction out of him. "You can't take him on your own."

"You underestimate us." The words rumbled from Rhodes.

"No! You underestimate Lysias. He thinks he is superior. He kills without remorse. Absolutely no regard for life."

"So do a lot of criminals," Johnson said gently.

"Not like Lysias." Kallie looked behind them again. A silver car drew her eye as it darted out of its lane into the next, then back in its lane, and over the line on the outside. She caught a flash of stark, white hair.

"We have a car coming up fast," Johnson said before she could.

"I see it," Rhodes responded. "Driving skills aren't much."

"It's Lysias."

"You sure?" Johnson asked, looking at her with a lot less doubt than before.

"Yes."

"Let's have a talk with this Lysias." Rhodes braked and started to pull to the side.

"No!" Kallie yelled.

Only to be drowned out by Johnson. "Look out. He's going to ram us."

Rhodes reacted immediately, pressing down on the gas.

The car shot forward, throwing Kallie back in the seat. She righted herself then was tossed to the side as Rhodes sent the car into a spin. She barely caught herself before slamming into the door. A hard jerk snapped her back the other way and had her straining against her seatbelt. The sound of crunching metal filled the car, then a jolt lifted her off the seat as they hit and went over the curb.

The car rocked and tilted. Kallie grabbed the door with one hand as she pressed her other to the roof. Afraid they were going to flip over, she tensed. Another jerk threw her forward then back into the seat as the car came to a rest, right side up.

It took a second for Kallie to calm her panic and realize she was all right, just shaken. Johnson sat between her and the caved-in door, his eyes closed. She reached to check him out and he stirred. Opening his eyes, he looked at her but seemed confused. Blood trickled down his face from a small cut on his forehead.

ଓଃ৪୦

The black vehicle slowed then picked up speed rapidly as if the driver finally figured out there was someone after him. Lysias charged toward the car.

Jerreon shifted, going for more speed, though there was no way he could intercept them in time. Lysias pulled up on the other vehicle. The driver of the black car braked and turned the wheel, sending the car into a controlled skid.

For a moment, Jerreon thought that Lysias was going to over-shoot them, but his car swerved, clipping the tail of the car, ramming it so it rocked violently. Hitting the curb, the black car jerked up and over. It started to tip on its side, threatening to flip until it impacted with a pole. With a tearing of metal, it dropped down onto the grass.

The car Lysias was in careened off, went through an intersection, barely missing several cars and nosed into a thick, tall palm tree.

Cars braked. People stared in shock at the accident.

Jerreon whipped to the side of the road and made his way around the congestion, almost to the wreck before he was forced to stop. He was out and running before the car had come to a rest.

He reached the government car first and jerked open the door. Kallie twisted in the seat. Relief flooded into her face at seeing him. "I'm all right," she stammered.

He reached for her, but she waved him off.

"Lysias."

She said the one thing that could get him to leave her. Still it tore at him.

"Go." She pressed out in his mind.

He knew it was her way of proving she was truly fine. Jerreon turned to the silver car resting twenty meters away. It was empty. For an instant, he was afraid he'd lost Lysias again, then he saw him trying to disappear into the crowd that had started to gather.

"Lysias!" Jerreon roared his name and ran after him.

The people blocking his way parted, letting him through.

Lysias didn't attempt to flee, but wrapped a hand around a small girl's arm, ripping the child from her mother. The woman screamed then fell to the ground as Lysias struck her with a backhanded blow. He turned and brought the girl in front of him as a shield.

People around them pulled back. Horror and fear filled the air.

Jerreon stopped ten feet from Lysias. "You would hide behind a child?"

"And you would risk yourself even to save one as insignificant as this?" Lysias countered. "Your humanity will get you killed."

"Your inhumanity condemns you."

"It is not inhumanity to know one's worth," Lysias snapped.

"Free the child."

Lysias shrugged. A smile curved his lips and he shoved the girl away. The smile disappeared as he brought the hand up, thrusting it out.

Energy flew at Jerreon in a bright blue ball. With so many people around, Jerreon knew he couldn't dodge and risk someone being hit, so he brought both hands up absorbing the energy into him. It crackled and burned his senses.

He clenched his teeth, and fought to maintain control, knowing if he lost it, for even a fraction of a second, it would singe him and he'd go down. He coursed the energy through his system. Taking a step closer to Lysias, he raised his hand to dispel some of the power racking his nerves.

Lysias pointed at the girl on the ground. "Stop, or the next one goes through the child. And you know she could not survive it."

"I will not let you."

"You cannot stop me. I am the most powerful being on this planet. You might have come close, but again your humanity hinders you." Lysias let out another burst of energy, sending it into the crowd.

Jerreon willed the energy to him. Agony etched through his already overloaded body. Gritting his teeth, he cycled the surge through him and right back out, sending it toward Lysias.

Lysias put his hands up but only in time to deflect the blast which hit his wrecked car, flipping the car onto its side. A second later, the car exploded into a fireball that had people screaming and pulling back even farther.

The explosion knocked Lysias to the ground, a shout of fear escaping him.

Jerreon raised an arm to protect his face until the flames died down. He rushed forward catching hold of Lysias's shirt, hauling him up to slam his fist into his face.

Lysias dropped, but Jerreon lifted him up ready to send another blow.

"No!" Jerreon heard Kallie scream and jerked around in time to see Kallie hit into one of the government men.

She knocked his hand holding a gun up just as a roar escaped it. A bullet ripped into a palm tree behind Jerreon, a couple feet above his head.

"That's my husband, you idiot," she shouted. "It's the other one you want."

Jerreon turned his attention back to Lysias, but the distraction cost him. Lysias locked a hand on his wrist and twisted to the side, clipping Jerreon's legs, taking them out from under him. Jerreon hit the ground beside Lysias, and the man rolled over on him, wrapping his hands around Jerreon's neck, squeezing down.

Jerreon thrust his hands up, breaking Lysias's hold, then slammed his palm into his chest, knocking Lysias away. Jerreon rolled to the side. They both gained their feet and attacked.

Lysias struck. Jerreon blocked and countered. Lysias blocked and kicked out. Jerreon turned away and continued the motion bringing his foot up in a sweeping arch that connected with Lysias's shoulder, knocking him back, but he didn't go down.

They circled each other, trading blows that didn't do any damage, just meant to wear their opponent down. Jerreon landed a hard blow that staggered Lysias. Lysias pulled back and glared. Jerreon felt the draw of energy and readied for the burst of power, but instead of being directed at him, Lysias again directed it to where the crowd had gathered across the street.

Jerreon leapt, covering the space to intersect the crackling ball of energy. The blast hit him in the chest throwing him back to land in the road. Pain burned through him as he tried to breathe. He thought he heard Kallie crying his name over the ringing in his ears.

Pain hit again as something touched his chest. Then, through the agony, he felt a gentle caress on his face. Stunned, he knew who it was, knew the touch and tried to cling to it.

He fought to clear his vision. He needed to sit up, move, but nothing in his body responded to the commands of his mind. Still, he managed to open his eyes and the glorious sight of Kallie filled his vision. He wanted to warn her away but couldn't move as energy continued to ricochet through his body.

The sound of a shot pierced his mind. Kallie jerked. Fear for her gave him enough strength to turn his head. He followed her gaze to see Lysias slash his hand against the air. The government man who had been in the car with Kallie and shot at him, fell back against the car. The gun in his hand ripped free to land a distance away as the man dropped to the ground.

Lysias's attention came back to them.

"Go," Jerreon choked on the word, but got it past his lips.

Kallie shifted, but didn't leave him. Kneeling by him, she held her head high as Lysias walked toward them.

Stopping, Lysias looked down. "As I said, your humanity is your downfall. I would have liked to have had you join me here, but I never could have trusted you. Besides, there should only be one god." He smirked.

"You are no god," Kallie snapped the words Jerreon wanted to say.

"Do you think you can withstand my power?" Lysias extended this hand out toward her.

"No!" Jerreon pulled himself up to a sitting position, placing himself in front of her.

"She does mean something to you." Lysias quirked up a brow. "It's not just the crystal that draws you to her."

"You want the crystal." Kallie reached for the fastener. "Take it and leave."

Before she could release the clasp, Lysias reached over Jerreon, caught her arm and jerked her up. "I want to know what makes you so special to him."

"No," Jerreon's cry echoed Kallie's as she fought to break Lysias's hold. Her protests were drowned out by the wail of approaching sirens.

"Stop," Lysias ordered pushing out his will, but it had no effect on her.

Jerreon saw the blow coming a split second before it contacted to her chin. Kallie went limp before his protest even made it out.

Lysias looked down the street at the cars with lights flashing on top, and hoisted Kallie over his shoulder.

"No." Jerreon tried to pull up, only to fall back as Lysias turned away. Pain threatened to shut him down and give his body the much needed healing time. Jerreon clung to the image of Lysias striding away with Kallie draped over his shoulder.

He rolled over and forced himself up to his hands and knees. The world swam around him. He let his head hang as he pulled air in his lungs to clear his mind before he forced his way to his feet. He staggered and almost went down again.

"You all right?"

He pulled his head up as several people dressed in some-kind of a uniform approached him, while others headed toward the government car. "Kallie, My one," he muttered. "My wife," he said more firmly, straightening.

"We'll see to her. Let's just get you sitting down first."

Another man moved to the car.

Jerreon ignored them forcing himself to take a step, then another. He staggered.

"Hey!" The man reached for him.

Jerreon heard the yell as he pushed himself into a run, taking off after Lysias. With each step, his systems leveled out. He pulled on the power, fueling his need to reach Kallie. He lengthened his stride. It took no effort to follow the trail.

He reached where the road crossed another larger street. The other side opened to the beach with the ocean stretching out. Jerreon barely glanced at the cars as he ran across the road amidst the blaring of horns. One car cut into his path and he hurtled it without slowing. People parted as he raced down the walk. He ignored their stares and shouts. His mind locked only on one thing – Kallie.

ନ୍ଧ

The jarring motion jerked Kallie back to consciousness. The world refused to right itself, and it took her a moment to realize her head was hanging down. Her hair almost skimmed the ground. A pathway and sand passed below her. She heard cars and waves. Under the noise, she made out the subtle sound of the ocean.

Lysias! Reality hit her and she started to fight. Striking his back, her hand stung. She kicked and squirmed trying to dislodge herself, but it only resulted in the arm clamped over her legs tightening down.

Pulling her head up, she caught an aghast expression on the face of an older aged couple, and the delighted expression on some young, teen-aged girls that obviously thought something romantic was happening. The thought freed her voice.

"Help! Please, call the police," she yelled. Kallie didn't want anyone to get hurt, but she also refused to go quietly. "Help!" She pushed up, then changed tactics and grabbed one of his legs.

Lysias went to step and she locked down on it hampering the motion. He staggered and his strength ripped the leg free from her, but she caught the other, impeding it so he stumbled. Kallie kicked and started to slide off his shoulder. He recovered, hoisted her back up then shook her, digging his shoulder into her stomach.

Kallie cried out.

"Hey!" a man called from behind them.

Kallie arched enough to see a couple guys in swim trunks heading their way.

"What's going on?" A sandy-haired guy demanded.

"Stay back or die." Contempt rang in Lysias's words.

Instead of halting, the men bristled.

It hit Kallie if she didn't do something, Lysias would kill them. She reached down, gripped his leg below the calf while she kicked up and arched her back, pulling with her arms. Half-turned, the action unbalanced them. Lysias dropped to the sand as she flipped over him to land flat on her back.

The sand took most of the impact, but she was lightheaded as she struggled to stand, only to fall again.

Fingers caught and locked around her wrist like steel-bands, dragging her to her feet. "Up." Lysias jerked her upright without giving her any option.

The guys rushed forward.

Lysias thrust out his free hand. Kallie slammed herself into him, knocking the hand away as a familiar blue-bolt burst from it. Energy hit the sand sending a spray of crystallized shards made from molten sand into the air.

Though the main force missed her, Kallie was so close tendrils of energy singed her. Lights flashed through her mind and vision and, for a moment, consciousness threatened to slip from her again.

Her mind cleared as she was dragged along, her legs barely able to keep her upright as they crossed the uneven sand, heading toward a small speed boat beached ahead. Kallie dug in, only to be yanked forward.

"Do not defy me again." Fury burned in his words.

She started to pull back only to be lifted up once more. A second later, Lysias waded into the water and dropped her into the boat.

Kallie landed, still stunned. The boat rocked, then a throaty roar rose from the engine. Over the sound, she thought she heard another roar.

"Jerreon," Kallie tried to pull herself up only to fall back as the boat lurched. Lysias spun the wheel nearly tipping the boat over when he goosed the engine at the same time. Kallie slid across the bottom of the boat to hit against the other side when he over corrected. Again, the world swam around her.

"My one!" Jerreon's call reached her and she clung to it, using it to hold her consciousness.

ᏩᎦᏴᎤ

Jerreon saw the flash of energy at the same time he felt the pull from the earth. Racing across the sand toward the area, he saw Lysias drop Kallie in a boat then vault in. The engine came to life, and he knew again he wasn't going to reach her in time to stop Lysias. His heart pounded. Energy still hummed in his system, but he couldn't pull on it to stop the boat, not with Kallie in it.

Two smaller crafts bobbed on the water not far away. He changed course heading for them. A man stood under an umbrella by a chair and a for rent sign.

"I need one of your crafts," Jerreon yelled as he approached. "My wife is being taken. How do I run this?"

"You don't know?" The man stepped in front of him.

Jerreon was already reaching out his mind for the information and caught the man's fear for his machine. He pulled out his wallet and tossed it to the man. "Hold this for my collateral and I will pay for it when I return it. There is a card in it. You can call to a man, if I do not return. He will pay for the machine. Now, how do I work it?"

Images flashed in the man's mind before the words made it out. Jerreon took them in. "Thank you." Jerreon freed the watercraft, pushing it out into the waves, igniting it in the same action as climbing on. Mashing down on the gas, it shot forward in an angle to cut Lysias off.

He reached his mind out for Kallie to assure himself she was all right. He felt her touch, but it didn't calm him.

Still, he was gaining rapidly on Lysias as the man struggled to control the boat.

Lysias twisted around, picking up his presence, and spun the boat sharply, cutting back toward him.

Jerreon let him come, meeting the challenge though the boat was twice the size of his own craft. Lysias arrowed in on him. Jerreon turned heading back to the beach. Lysias followed, gaining on him, aiming at running him over.

CSSO

Kallie gripped the side of the boat and pulled herself up. Stumbling when the boat hit a rough patch, she almost went down, and then she saw Jerreon. The sun gleamed off his now sandy hair so the white of it appeared to shine through. He stood, letting his legs take the pounding of the waves as he sped across the water.

Lysias turned the wheel sharply, almost knocking her over as he headed right for Jerreon, in a clear attempt to run him down.

Kallie dove forward, grabbing for the handle that controlled the gas. She yanked it back to stop position as she reached for the wheel. The boat hit a wave just as the engine cut off and she whipped the wheel around. The boat spun and nosed down in the water in a violent action. The momentum ripped Kallie's hand from the wheel at the same time Lysias struck her, sending her flying over the side into the water, landing a good ten feet away.

The impact felt like she hit into a brick wall, then she was sinking into the fluid depths. Panic jarred her stunned mind back to alertness. She struggled and fought as the water closed over her. In her panic, it took a second to right herself and determine which way was up.

Straightening out her body, she pulled the water with her arms as she kicked her way to the surface. She broke through gasping in air and choking out salt water. The roar of a motor had her turning in time to see Jerreon bring the personal watercraft in close to the boat, and leap onboard.

She could only tread water and watch as the two men locked on each other in death grips.

Kallie was so absorbed in the struggle, she almost missed the gray fin that cut through the surface in front of her, until it dipped and disappeared back in the water. Fear filled her so fast she couldn't scream or react.

Chapter Fourteen

Something bumped her side. Kallie shrieked. In answer, a smooth gray head with a long nose broke the surface and chattered back to her.

Kallie sagged in relief, dipping in the water. The dolphin moved into her, not shying back when she slipped her arm over it. She tried to shift to watch Jerreon, but the dolphin turned, dragging her toward shore. Kallie slipped off only to have another brush along her. Out of instinct, she caught hold of the fin as she'd seen the trainers in the park do.

The dolphin carried her toward shore with three others forming a protective ring around her. They were in only about two and a half feet of water when they pulled up and flipped around, leaving her kneeling on the sandy bottom as waves rocked her. Kallie remained there, drawing in air, watching the fight a couple hundred feet away.

"No," a scream burst from her as something touch her. She swung her arm out only to have it caught. A lifeguard and another man pulled her to her feet and dragged her in the final feet to shore.

"That was amazing," the man exclaimed.

"Something I've never seen before. You're all right?" the lifeguard asked trying to draw her attention.

Kallie ignored him focusing on the fight as the sound of blows crashed over the water. She could only watch helplessly as Jerreon and Lysias locked together. She knew only one would make it to shore alive – maybe neither.

⊂∞⊃

Jerreon kept his focus on Lysias, but it was hard knowing Kallie was in the water, possibly hurt. Even though he had the assurance from the dolphins that had answered his call, he wanted to reach out to Kallie, but couldn't risk the distraction.

Lysias swung at him. Jerreon blocked, ramming his fist in Lysias's side. The boat rocked hampering the strength behind the blow, but still Lysias staggered before coming in.

Lysias struck, feinting to the side in an attempt to draw him off. Jerreon caught the movement and countered in time to take the blow with his shoulder. Pain seared up his arm as Lysias connected where the bullet from the police officer's gun had grazed him.

Jerreon gasped and faltered in his blow, leaving him open for Lysias to land another hit to his ribs. Air exploded from his body, followed by the flare of pain from the rib cracking. Still, Jerreon continued his counter strike, clipping Lysias in the face with enough force to snap Lysias's head back. Jerreon was rewarded with the sound of cartilage popping. Blood spurt from Lysias's nose.

Lysias roared, diving in, throwing fists wildly, all done to get close enough to wrap his hands around Jerreon's neck. Jerreon drove his fist up, breaking the hold, knocking Lysias back against the front of the boat. Again, the boat rocked wildly.

Jerreon, his feet spread wide, rode out the motion.

Lysias fell against the side of the boat, gripping the edge to keep from going over.

Jerreon reached to pull him up.

Lysias sprang, slashing out his hand. Light flashed off a knife blade.

Jerreon pulled back an instant too late. The blade meant for his heart hit one of his ribs then sunk in where the rib had broken a moment before. Agony dropped him to his knees. He gripped his side and struggled to stand, teetering at the back of the boat.

"I will be god here," Lysias shouted in exaltation, bringing both hands in front of him. Energy balled and crackled from his hands. Lysias roared again. Power burst out.

Jerreon thrust up his hands, willing his own energy out. The two bursts collided in an explosion of hot, blue-white energy, scorching through Jerreon as he was thrown backward into the water.

ഇൻ

Kallie ducked and shaded her eyes at the flash of light. "Jerreon!" she screamed, then cried again as the boat exploded. Helpless she watched Jerreon's body be thrown back. It landed in the water, sinking below the waves. "Jerreon!"

She ran into the water only to be stopped by one of the men who helped pull her to shore a moment earlier. "Please let me go. I have to get to him." She fought to get free, but he held her arms trapped against her body and dragged her back out of the surf. Another person joined him and pulled her up on the shore.

"Help's on the way."

The lifeguard who pulled her out and another ran past her into the water.

"The dolphins!" someone shouted.

Kallie saw several fins rise to the surface. In the midst of them was a form.

"Jerreon." Her mind went out to him, but all she met with was quiet. Terror filled her like it never had before. "No, Jerreon!" She put more will into her effort and reached again to touch his mind.

A second passed, then a slight stirring. He was alive. Jerreon didn't answer, but she knew.

Tears burned her eyes as she watched. In tandem, one on either side of Jerreon, the dolphins nudged him toward the beach. The lifeguards stopped, standing in waist deep water as the dolphins brought Jerreon into them, releasing him once they reached the humans. This time, the dolphins didn't pull back from the shore. They circled in the shallows letting out volleys of high-pitched whistles.

The man holding her let go, and she waded into the water to meet the men carrying Jerreon in. Water whisked away blood from dozens of cuts showing through his shredded clothes. Kallie caught a cry behind her hand at the sight of a knife protruding from his side.

"No, Jerreon." She grasped a leg helping to lift him as there was nothing else she could do.

The man with her took the other side, and together with the lifeguards, they all carried him up the beach where a blanket had been laid out and rescue workers waited.

It wasn't until then she realized how many people had gathered around. Police and rescuers dotted the beach. Government people in dark pants with white polo-shirts mingled among them giving orders to keep people back. Kallie took it all in, then turned her attention back to Jerreon.

Keeping a hand on his leg, she dropped to the ground as they lowered him down. Tears slipped free as she fought for calm, afraid any moment she would be forced away. She tried not to focus on the knife in his side, but the sight of it held her.

Blood seeped down his side. She wanted them to rid him of the offending protrusion, but figured it was best to leave it there until they got him to the hospital. The paramedics must have decided the same thing because they packed the wound to stabilize the knife.

Kallie could only pray what they were doing to him would be okay for his body. Jerreon had told her they had identical physical make-up. He'd said it to assure her when they had a child all would be well.

She caught back a cry. Still, a tear slipped free to trickle down her cheek. She may never get to hold his baby. "Jerreon," she whispered his name, repeating it in her mind, sending it out to his.

His chest rose as he pulled in a breath. His eyes fluttered.

"He's coming around," someone said.

Jerreon's gaze moved around the people. Panic coming off him touched her. Kallie rose up to her knees, stroking her fingers over his calf. His eyes met hers. She felt his relief.

"My one," he whispered the words behind the oxygen mask that had been placed over his face. Kallie felt them in her heart.

"My one," she repeated back.

"It is done. Lysias is gone."

Relief hit her only to disappear as he tightened in pain. "My pack?" Before she could answer, he stiffened slightly then went limp.

"Jerreon," she cried out. Her eyes went to the patch visible on his arm where he'd been shot earlier that day. He'd said it would be healed by tomorrow. She needed to get to his backpack, to the healing pads he had.

"Let's get him loaded," one of the paramedics said.

Kallie was forced back as they lifted Jerreon onto a stretcher. His feet hung off the end. But that was only part of the reality of the situation. It was impossible for her to fathom Jerreon injured.

Kallie went to follow him only to be stopped by a hand on her arm. "Mrs. Ander," one of the agents said her name. Rigby, it took a moment to remember his name.

She tried again to follow the men loading Jerreon in the back of the ambulance, but he held her back. "We'll take you to the hospital. We have some questions."

"I want to go with my husband." She pulled away, but before she could take a step, the doors on the ambulance closed, cutting off her view.

"As I said, we'll take you," the man said forcefully from behind her.

She turned to glare, but the intent of action was ruined as dizziness swamped her, and she almost fell.

The next thing Kallie knew, she was seated on the ground and one of the paramedics was shining a light in her eyes. "Can you tell me how you got the bump on your head?"

Kallie raised her hand only to have it caught and brought back down to her lap, but not before she realized the side of her head hurt.

"I'm not sure, either the car accident or when Lysias hit me, maybe on the boat." She tried to think back, but so much had happened. All she wanted was the backpack and to get to Jerreon.

"Were you on the boat when it blew up?" the woman taking her blood pressure asked.

"No. Please, my husband."

"The man they just took away?"

"Yes, I need to get to him."

"Don't worry. They're doing everything they can. His vitals looked good. We'll get you to the hospital to be checked out. You may have a concussion. We'll have to wait for another ambulance though."

"I don't need an ambulance. I just want to get to the hospital."

"You should be checked out." The paramedic reasoned with her.

"We'll take her and see she's taken care of."

Kallie hadn't noticed Agent Rigby standing beside her. The paramedic looked up and nodded. Obviously, the government man was pulling his weight.

With the paramedic's help, Kallie stood. Rigby took her arm, urging her toward the road where several black cars were parked. Halfway to the vehicles another agent intercepted them.

"If you'll wait here a moment, then we'll go." Rigby instructed, moving off with Truman.

Kallie looked around, but figured there was no way she could get to the hospital on her own, so she waited.

"What'd they find?"

Kallie could easily make out Rigby's question.

"There's no sign of the other guy. There's blood and a couple big sharks in the water. I mean real big sharks. We don't dare send divers down right now. They appear highly agitated."

Kallie looked up and down the beach, then over the water. There were two boats where the other had been when it exploded. Pieces of debris were starting to wash up on the shore. What she didn't see was any signs of Lysias.

"It's done. Lysias is gone." Jerreon's words came back to her.

Even though Lysias was as evil as he was, she hoped he was gone when he went into the water. She shivered at the memory of the fear she'd experienced before she realized it was a dolphin that bumped into her. Then the thought of a bleeding Jerreon in the water hit her. The need to get to him filled her stronger than ever.

Kallie looked around for a way to leave, but she didn't know where the hospital was. She didn't have her cell phone. Johnson had taken it, and for that matter, she didn't even know where the car was. She also didn't have her purse. She guessed it was still in the government car. Mainly, she needed Jerreon's pack and the medicine patches in it.

The paramedics were loading gear back into their vehicle. "Excuse me." She approached the woman who had checked her out. "Can you tell me what hospital my husband was taken to?"

"That's not necessary Mrs. Ander. We're ready to leave now." Agent Rigby came up behind her.

The paramedic did a slight shrug, which Kallie interpreted as 'there isn't anything I can do'.

"Thank you," Kallie said before turning to the agent.

A minute later, she found herself in the back of another black car. This time Agent Rigby was at the wheel. Agent Truman had joined them and was sitting in the back with her.

"Have you heard anything of Jerreon?" she asked as soon as they pulled away from the curb.

"Just that they've reached the hospital," Agent Truman answered her.

Ahead Kallie saw the remnants of the crash Lysias caused. "How are Johnson and Rhodes?"

"They've been taken to the hospital to be checked out."

"Is it possible to get my purse and phone out of the car?" Kallie saw the two agents exchanged glances then Truman nodded.

"Stay in the car," Rigby said as he pulled the car to a stop.

"I also need my backpack that's in Jerreon's car. Over there." She pointed and held her breath. If they figured the pack was Jerreon's, she was sure they would confiscate it.

Rigby got out and went to talk to a couple other people at the scene before going to the wrecked car. He reached in the back and pulled her bag then, to her relief, she caught a glimpse of her cell phone before he dropped it in the bag. He next walked to the sports car and leaned in, snagging up Jerreon's pack. Kallie watched him stare at it a second before he headed back. He climbed in before handing it over the seat to her.

"Thank you," she said, hugging the bags to her. She wanted to call Adam, but knew it would be better to wait to be alone first.

"Can you tell us what happened back there?" Truman's question took her by surprise, cutting through the silence in the car.

"Lysias tried to kidnap me." She went for the simple truth. "He ran us off the road."

"Who exactly is this Lysias?" Rigby asked.

"All I know is he's a criminal."

"And your husband was after him?" Rigby pressed.

Pain slashed at Kallie, along with the image of the knife imbedded in Jerreon's side. "Actually, I would say Lysias was after him." She fought to hold back her cry. "He's the one who came after me. To use me against Jerreon." The sob slipped free. "I'd like to rest." She turned her head to look out the window though she didn't see anything.

"Mrs. Ander, witnesses said it was like they were throwing lightening at each other. How did your husband do that?" Truman pressed.

She looked at the woman. "I don't know what you're talking about, but I don't feel good." Kallie closed her eyes. Letting her mind drift out, she tried to feel Jerreon though she knew it was useless, still the need for him pulled her to try. Her call echoed back in the dark void.

Tears threatened again to wash over her as ocean water had moments before. *"Jerreon. My one."* She wrapped her fingers around the crystal and cried out in one more futile attempt.

A brief flash of blue sparked in her mind. A faint glow of awareness touched her. Jerreon was close. She clung to the knowledge and it grew stronger. Kallie opened her eyes to find them pulling around the hospital. She reached for the door handle as they came to a stop, but it was locked.

Neither agent said anything as they helped her out and led her in. Truman waited with her while Rigby talked with a man at the admitting desk. A minute later, Kallie was taken directly back into an exam room and left there with Agent Truman.

"Am I being detained?" she asked when the woman leaned back against the wall and folded her arms.

"No, I'm just waiting with you."

"Please, can you find out about Jerreon?"

"Agent Rigby will let us know if there is any word."

Kallie sank down in a chair, closed her eyes and attempted to feel for Jerreon again. He was there in the back of her senses, but it wasn't the strong vibrant presence she'd come to know.

A moment later a doctor entered. He looked at her briefly and asked for x-rays. When he left an aid came in with a wheelchair. Truman remained at her side all the way down the hall, but was forced to wait outside while Kallie was wheeled to radiology.

"The tech will be with you in a minute," the man said before leaving her alone.

Kallie could see a woman in a small room off to the side, but took the opportunity to pull out her phone.

"Kallie," Adam answered immediately.

"Thank heavens. I don't think I have long. We're at the hospital. Jerreon's hurt. Lysias came after me, and they fought. Lysias is gone, but he stabbed Jerreon, then the boat they were fighting on blew up. Jerreon's alive, but I don't know how he is. They haven't let me see him."

"How are you?" Adam asked when she stopped to breathe.

Tears caught in her throat. "They think I have a concussion, but I'm fine. I'm just afraid. They won't let me to him. There are a lot of agents here. They're asking questions about him." She saw the woman stand. "I have to go. Someone's coming."

"I'll be right there," Adam said right before she disconnected.

Kallie sagged, relief leaving her weak and shaking.

"Not feeling well?" the woman said in way of greeting as she approached.

Kallie looked up and blinked. "I just haven't been able to find out anything about my husband. I'm so worried."

The woman frowned. "Did you come in at the same time?"

Kallie felt maybe she had an ally. "They brought him first. He'd been stabbed." Her voice trembled saying the words.

"Big guy. Real good looking?"

"Yes," Kallie let out. "Jerreon Ander."

"I handled his x-ray. They wanted a full scan on him, but all I saw was a broken rib. Let me call the nurse and see what I can find out." The tech went back to the other room. Kallie watched her through the glass as she picked up the phone.

The tech came back a minute later. "They're being real hush about him. All I could find out is, they have him stitched up and have moved him into a room for recovery."

Kallie sagged in relief. "Will they let me see him then?"

"You'll have to talk with one of the doctors. I don't know what's going on." It was obvious what was happening had perplexed her.

"Thank you so much."

She smiled. "Let's get your x-rays."

Kallie was finished in a few minutes and taken back to an exam room with Agent Truman following. "Can you tell me about my husband?" Kallie broke the tomb-like silence that filled the room. "Please," she added when the agent didn't look at her.

The woman glanced her way. "I'm sorry. I haven't been made aware of any information." A look of annoyance passed over her. "Someone else is taking over."

What did that mean? Who would be taking over? Kallie didn't like it. She reached for Jerreon and felt a weak contact, but he didn't acknowledge her, which heightened her fear. He would've been medicated, she tried to reason. Perhaps that was why she couldn't reach him.

Standing, Kallie paced the small room, her gaze going to Jerreon's pack. With Truman in the room, she didn't dare go through it. She also didn't dare use her phone again, afraid they might take it from her. She was on at least her hundredth lap around the room when a cell phone chirped in an annoying upbeat, popular song.

Truman pulled the device out. "Yes," the woman answered and a second later stepped out of the room.

Kallie followed her to the door, but when she pulled on it, it wouldn't budge. She smacked her hand against the offending obstruction, then leaned her head against it as dizziness swept over her.

Jerreon, she cried in her mind, but no answer came, just a bone chilling emptiness. After a moment, she made her way back to the exam table and settled down. Closing her eyes, she brought up a clear image of Jerreon, but her mind felt too muddled to reach for him again.

A few minutes later, a doctor finally came in and told her she was being released, but cautioned her to take things easy for a couple days.

"What about my husband?"

"Sorry, I have no information about him. Try asking at the desk." He left the room, not giving her a chance to press, and a nurse came in to wheel her out. Agent Truman was not waiting in the hall. There was no sign of the government people.

"Kallie," Adam called her name as she came through the doors. Kallie scrambled out of the wheelchair and ran to him. He circled her in his arms. The tears she'd been fighting flooded out.

"How's Jerreon?" he asked when her crying eased.

"I don't know. They haven't let me see him yet or won't even tell me anything." Another sob escaped her.

"Let me see what I can find out." He patted her hand then led her to the desk. He waited for the woman there to give him her attention. "I'm hoping you can help us. We're trying to find out about my nephew. His wife was just released, but she hasn't been given any information about him and would like to go back and see him."

"His name?"

"Jerreon Ander," Kallie answered first.

"A-N-D-E-R." The woman spelled the name.

"Yes, J-E R-R-E-O-N." Kallie supplied.

"I show no record of anyone by the name of Ander." The woman looked up. "Maybe he was taken somewhere else."

"He was brought here. We both were by Homeland Security."

The woman blinked in surprise, obviously she'd heard of something. "Let me call my supervisor."

A moment later, a slightly haggard looking woman came up to the desk. "May I help you?"

"Yes," Kallie burst out. "I'd like to see my husband."

"Easy," Adam said softly, patting her hand. "We'd like to see my nephew. This is his wife, and she hasn't been able to find out anything."

"I'm afraid he isn't here," the woman said.

"Don't tell me that. I know they brought him here." Kallie gripped the counter, her body trembling with tension. "He was unconscious. He had a knife wound and a broken rib."

"Yes, well, I know nothing of that. I just know he was not admitted and is gone."

"Gone? How?" Adam squeezed down on Kallie's hand, taking over the questioning.

"I don't know the details. I'm sorry." The woman started to back away. "He's not here."

"Can I talk to Agent Rigby or Truman, please? Can you call them for me?" Kallie asked before she could leave.

"All the agents have left." The woman twisted her hands, clearly agitated.

"What about agents Johnson and Rhodes? I was told they were brought in with injuries to be checked out," Kallie tried again.

"I'm afraid I can't give out any information to a non-relative." She stiffened.

"I am a relative. I want to see my husband," Kallie cried.

"Your husband isn't here, and if you're going to make a scene, I'm afraid I'll have to call security." The woman turned and disappeared back through the door, leaving the other woman at the desk looking helpless.

"Come on." Adam slipped his arm around her waist and directed Kallie away. She went with him several feet then froze, wrapping her hand around the crystal. Once more she reached for Jerreon. There was nothing.

"He's gone. They've taken him." Kallie covered her mouth, holding back a sob, then buried her face in her hands and cried.

Adam wrapped his arm around her and guided her through the door to a bench outside.

Kallie sank down, no longer able to hold herself up. "Jerreon," she cried out in pain for the part of her that was missing.

Adam held her close. "Don't give up yet. Let me call in a few favors and see if I can't find something." He comforted after her breakdown had passed.

Kallie gulped back a sob. "But Adam, what will they do to him?"

"Now don't think about that. They won't hurt him. I'm sure of it. They'd be foolish to." He patted her hand again. His limo pulled up in front of them. Adam drew her up and into the plush vehicle.

Back at his estate, he walked her to her room and told her to rest while he tried to find out what he could. Kallie sank down on the bed she'd shared with Jerreon just hours before. She wrapped her arms around his pillow. His lingering scent filled her, setting free tears until exhaustion took her, and she slept.

The sun was setting when she woke. Kallie stepped out on the balcony and looked down at the garden where, just the evening before, she'd married Jerreon. It seemed eons ago. Steadying herself she went to find Adam, aware if he'd found out anything he would have come to tell her.

He was at his desk. For the first time, he looked harried. His snowy white hair was in disarray from running his fingers through it. He stood when she entered, coming to wrap his arms around her. They held each other.

"I haven't been able to find anything." Her pain echoed in him. He, too, had come to care about Jerreon in just the short time.

Kallie nodded, hugging him back, willing comfort to him, as she took in his strength.

After a moment, they released each other.

"Why don't we go try to eat something? Lucille's been holding it for us." Together they went out to the deck where the table sat waiting. Dinner didn't hold the pleasure it had the night before, but Kallie forced herself to eat. It wouldn't do Jerreon any good if she got sick.

"Your family has made it home safely. I figured you'd still want to know that, at least, until we get this all figured out."

"Yes." Kallie wanted her family, but really couldn't face having them there right then either. All she wanted was Jerreon.

Adam laid a hand on hers. "Sam is trying some of his old contacts in national security. We're not giving up."

Kallie nodded, managed a few more bites before giving up and excusing herself to wander out through the garden. She let her mind drift to the faint sounds of waves that reached her. Gripping the railing, she looked over the ocean. She picked up a stirring of awareness. For a moment she hoped it was Jerreon, but as she followed it out, she came in contact with a pod of dolphins just off the shore.

As earlier, she couldn't tell what they were saying, just they were there. *"Thank you,"* she sent gratitude out to them. They had saved her and Jerreon. Warmth came back, along with whistles and a consoling calm, then they were gone.

Kallie made her way back to Adam's library, curling into a chair, half-listening while Adam and his security went over their options.

She wasn't aware of Adam until he touched her shoulder. "Why don't you get some sleep? It's almost midnight. We'll start again early."

Kallie looked around and realized the other two men were gone.

"We all need some rest," he said gently.

Kallie nodded and made it to her feet. The room swam around her. Adam caught her arm steadying her.

"I'm okay," Kallie assured, but let him lead her up the stairs.

At her room, he said good-night. Kallie looked around, not really wanting to be there. Not without Jerreon. She went to the bed, but couldn't yet force herself to lie down. She wandered around a minute before going into the bathroom and turning on the shower.

The first sob hit her as she stepped under the spray. Tilting her head up, she let the water carry away her tears. She collapsed against the shower wall, letting the water beat down on her. The water started to chill before she reached over and turned it off. The thick towels she'd admired that morning held no pleasure as she dried.

Working the brush through her hair reminded her of Jerreon running his fingers through it. He seemed to like the feel. She liked his hair also, and wanted to see it; not how it had been today, but his natural white-blond. That was the way he looked in her mind. How he'd been on the beach when he first touched her cheek and claimed her as his.

"My One," she repeated the words. "I will find you."

Her gaze landed on Jerreon's pack. Earlier it had seemed important. Kallie sat on the bed opening it. She really didn't hope to find anything that would lead her to him, it was just – his.

On top was his bloody shirt. Tears started to flow with her fear. He'd been hurt so much today – shot, stabbed, and she didn't know what else in the explosion.

She felt pain deep in her and wondered if it was hers or his. He'd said something once about being able to share pain. She wanted to share his pain, give him her strength, whatever he needed.

She forced herself to continue through the pack. He'd taken out much of what was in it, like the coins which were in Adam's safe. There were several things she didn't know what they were, but the case she found interested her. It took several tries to figure out how to open it.

Several small tubes with strange symbols on them held different colored tablets. There were bandages like he'd placed on his arm in different sizes. Kallie couldn't help but wonder if they really could heal him. She wished she'd asked him more about them. Closing the case, she put it in her purse. She would find him.

A wave of dizziness hit her. For now, she needed rest. She lay back and reached for his pillow, hugging it tight, but once more it didn't replace the man she loved.

What was happening to him? Fear assaulted her with the images of old movies. Government man hunts. Scientists dissecting aliens alive. She tried to force them away reasoning that they wouldn't do anything like that. But Kallie couldn't get past the point that he'd been taken after people had seen Jerreon do things there was no explanation for.

All she could do was pray he was safe. Her mind couldn't grip the possibility he was dead. No – she'd know if he was.

Chapter Fifteen

Kallie struggled through the surf, searching for Jerreon. She knew he was there, just out of her reach, trapped, strapped to a table in a cold vault. Gray walls hid the people watching him. Machines monitored everything from the breaths he took to every little blip of his brain. He floated in a haze of pain.

He reached for her as if sensing her, but the tendrils of his will petered out before she could grab them.

"No!" Kallie called coming awake. Her heart pounded. She bit down on her lip to keep from crying out again. She had to find Jerreon. Climbing from the bed, she pulled on the first clothes she found.

The house was silent as she stepped out of the room. It was early still. Kallie headed downstairs not knowing what she could do, but she had to do something. When she pushed open the double doors to the library, she found Adam and two of his security men at the desk.

"Kallie." Adam rose to come to her. He didn't ask how she slept or try to placate her. He just drew her forward. "So far, we still haven't found anything. There's not a peep from anyone willing to talk about Jerreon." He settled her in the chair.

"We're waiting to hear from an old friend of Sam's, but it isn't looking promising," he continued. "Josh has been surfing some alien theorist watch sites. That has yielded more than anything. Someone even has a video of the fight between Jerreon and Lysias. It's going viral. Speculation is running rampant if it's a hoax or real. That it's real seems to be winning."

He gave her a half smile. "Theory has it the government is covering up. Have to agree there. The guys are checking out a couple names and places that are popping up that they think they might take him to, that is, if there is any truth to these sites."

Sam nodded to her. "We'll find him."

"That was quite a show they put on." Josh spoke up. "The news guys tried to get on it, but all they got from the official report was an explosion of a stolen boat and a shark attack."

Kallie wondered how much they knew of Jerreon. She thought Sam, at least, knew it all.

"I forgot to tell you," Adam said. "A man called yesterday. He had Jerreon's wallet. Jerreon took his personal watercraft and left the wallet with him. Sam picked it up."

"The craft had been returned to him without any explanation," Sam added.

"There's nothing else we can do?" Kallie felt beat.

"As I said, we'll find him," Sam repeated. Hard lines furrowed his features. He was a man accustomed to challenges and winning. That was what he did and why Adam would've hired him.

She nodded. "I'm going to get some air."

"That's a good idea. I'll have breakfast sent out," Adam said.

Kallie wanted to say not to bother, but knew she had to eat. A minute later, she found herself back at the railing over the surf, reaching out for Jerreon. Nothing met her call. She wished the dolphins back for just a touch of connection, but there was no link from them either.

She stood for a moment, letting the morning sun shine down on her, but it did nothing to warm her. If she didn't find Jerreon soon, Kallie figured she'd freeze and dry up inside, not that it mattered. She couldn't go on with half of her missing. The worst thing was, she didn't have any idea how to go about finding him.

"Kallie," Adam called her. "Come eat."

Too grateful for his help to do anything to add to his worry, she joined the men at the patio table. Kallie picked at her food while they ate.

"I've found three locations that seem to keep popping up like an Area 51 type thing," Josh said between bites. "The first is a lake just a little inland from here. It's supposed to have alien ties. It's thought to have a government facility there to monitor the activity. Next is on the coast just north of here. Officially, they do tidal research, but on the loops, they say it has more to do with earth energy mapping and alien stuff. The other location is farther out in the desert."

Kallie tried to follow the idea of it all, but it seemed so out there, then again, Jerreon made 'out there' feel not so far away.

"Josh and I thought it might not be a bad idea to go check out the first location, since that's where the highest amount of speculation indicates," Sam said. "If that doesn't pan out, we'll move on to the next."

"Agreed. Go. Just keep in touch," Adam said.

The men stood and left the table.

"Maybe I should go with them." Kallie started to rise.

Adam caught her hand and pulled her back down. "Not yet. Let them check it out first."

"But if I get close enough, I might be able to feel him." Emotion made her voice waver.

"If I let anything happen to you, Jerreon would never forgive me."

"But −"

"You are the most important thing to him. Even over his own life. Trust me on this. I know. He wouldn't want you in danger."

"He's the most important thing to me," she cried, choking on the words.

"I know dear, just be patient. Give them a chance. If they can find anything, we'll start driving. We'll cover the whole country if we have to."

Kallie sank back into the chair. Covering her face with her hands, she nodded.

Silence settled over them.

Kallie sat with her arms wrapped around herself as if to help hold herself together. She didn't know how many times the hum brushed across her senses before it registered. She reached out with her mind and listened.

Excitement hit her. It took a second to make out it was the dolphins offshore once more. She started to pull back from them when urgency joined the emotions hitting her.

Jerreon! The thought came to her clear again with another wave of excitement. And she knew – they'd found him.

Kallie sprang to her feet, knocking over the chair. "I've got to go."

"What?" Adam jerked up.

"Jerreon." She pulled back. "I can find him. The dolphins. Can I borrow a car?"

"I'm going with you. Let me get Edward." He had his phone out already. Not questioning her, he hit a button. "Meet us at the car," he said without preamble.

"I need my purse." Kallie ran into the house, taking the stairs two at a time. She snatched up the bag from where she had left it the night before, glanced inside to make sure Jerreon's medical kit was there before running back down the stairs.

Adam held the door of the limo for her, following her as she dove inside.

"Where to?" Edward asked, waiting in the driver's seat.

"North, along the coast," she answered. No one said anything as tension filled the car.

They angled away from the shore pulling out of the neighborhood, and for a moment Kallie thought she'd lost the connection, but as soon as they closed back to the ocean, the dolphins were there waiting.

Ten minutes passed. Adam called Sam to tell them what they were doing. Ten more minutes went by.

"Are we still good?" Edward asked.

"Yes." Excitement poured off the dolphins now, plain for her to read. Strengthened now, she picked up a familiar awareness. Jerreon. They were getting closer. She reached for him knowing she was touching him, but he didn't answer.

I'm coming. She pressed out the words along with her love. A few minutes later, the dolphins stopped just off the shore.

"Slow down." Kallie cried. He was close now, but he seemed muted to her. "There." She pointed to a driveway between two mounds decorated with rocks, pampas grass and flowering plants.

Another fifty feet, and it opened up to a circular drive. In the center of which was a huge, metal sculpture that looked like stylized waves. Behind it rose several large concrete buildings built into the rocky cliff, extending out over the water. Another structure jutted up in the surf.

"Jerreon's here."

"Pull over and park," Adam told Edward.

Kallie climbed out before the limo came to a complete stop.

"Kallie wait," Adam called, getting out after her. "We go in there together. You do realize they probably won't just hand him over."

"I'm not leaving without him." Kallie turned to the entrance, feeling the pull in her heart, but she waited as Adam stopped to talk to Edward.

"Stay here and call Sam. Let him know where we're at." Adam turned to take her arm.

Kallie realized Adam had a cane with him. She'd only seen him carry the thing a couple times. He used it for effect when he was in a serious mood. He entered the building like he owned the place. The tip of the cane tapped the floor loudly. Adam was ready for battle.

The doors opened automatically to a large room with high ceilings. Mosaic tiles put together in an abstract picture of the ocean and its waves cresting, covered one wall. Another wall held a floor to ceiling window looking out over the rocky shore where the waves crashed. Displays were set around the room depicting waves, wind and sun. A round steel and tile reception desk sat in front of them with the word 'information' hanging above it.

Adam only paused slightly before heading to the desk. "We'd like to see the supervisor in charge," he said to the woman at the desk.

"I'm sorry. Mr. Harmon is tied up in meetings. I'm afraid we're not giving tours today, though you are free to look around the displays here in the lobby," the attendant said with canned sweetness.

"We're not interested in a tour. We'd like to speak to someone in charge here." Adam's voice remained courteous even though Kallie heard the steel in it.

The receptionist must've too, because she became quite defensive in her tone. "I'm afraid that's not possible."

"Please, we need to speak to someone." Kallie stepped forward, placing her hands on the counter to keep from reaching across to grip the receptionist's arm.

The receptionist took a step back, her hand disappearing under the counter.

"I'm looking for my husband," Kallie said leaning in.

That seemed to take the woman by surprise, but before she could say anything, a middle-aged, balding man in a white lab coat strode toward the desk.

"May I help you?" he asked looking them over, his lips tightening in a firm line.

"Yes," Adam stepped forward. "We're looking for Jerreon Ander."

"There is no one here by that name." He turned and started to walk away.

Kallie crossed the space that separated them in four strides. Reaching out, she caught his arm. At the same height, she halted him easily. "You're lying. He is here. Jerreon Ander. He's a tall man, seven feet, blond hair. He's kind of hard to miss, especially since he was injured."

"Let go of me." He looked down at her hand. "Or I will call security."

Kallie straightened. "I want to see him now. Where is he?"

The doctor pulled back, looking indignant. "You're mistaken. Why would an injured man be brought here? We're an institute devoted to tidal research." He pulled his arm free, straightening his cuff.

"That might be your cover, but there's a lot more going on here." She stepped forward, all her fear turning to anger.

The doctor backed away and a burly man in a guard uniform came hurrying across the floor, stepping in between them, grabbing her wrist.

Kallie pulled back but was caught. "Let me go."

"See them out." The balding man huffed.

"No." Kallie started to fight.

The guard wrapped one of his thick arms around her waist lifting her off the ground.

"Let me go."

Adam moved to her assistance, as all the other people in the room stopped and stared. Several guards appeared through side doors. One cut Adam off before he could reach her. Another grabbed her other arm as she slipped free.

"Have them arrested," the man in charge ordered.

"No!" Kallie twisted trying to break away but was held firm. "Jerreon!" she yelled at the top of her lungs. "Let me go. Jerreon!" She felt a shift in her awareness. "Jerreon. Where is he? He is here."

Kallie rammed an elbow into the stomach of the last man to arrive, forcing the air from him. He stumbled back. She tried to pull away from the other man, but he held on, twisting her arm higher.

Kallie cried out as pain spiked in her. She started to drop to her knees, but an arm like a steel band wrapped around her waist, squeezing the air from her. Everything started to haze over in her mind.

A groan rumbled up from the ground under them, and the floor shook.

Everyone froze, looking around.

"Earthquake!" Several people cried out.

"Jerreon!" Kallie screamed.

"Stop that!" the man in charge snapped.

A second later, a small man with his white lab coat flapping around him burst into the room, panic flushed on his face. "He's awake," the man gasped. "We don't know what happened. One minute we were losing him. The next —" The little man looked back over his shoulder, his eyes wide, breathing rapidly. "It's not going to hold him." His voice climbed several octaves.

There was another rumble. The floor quivered. A grinding screech, like fingernails on a chalkboard, rent the air. A thunderous bang shook the building.

Everyone jumped.

"Stay calm," the man in charge ordered, but it had little effect.

Everyone turned to the two swinging metal doors.

Stillness filled the air with baited breath. The door swung out, banging back against the wall and stayed open.

A second later, Jerreon strode through the opening. Ramrod straight, barefoot, wearing only a pair of boxers and a bandage wrapped around his waist. A sheen of sweat gleamed on the wide expanse of his chest. Energy crackled in the air around him. His hands were fisted at his sides delineating his muscles. His eyes blazed with fury.

"Release my wife." His demand split the air, echoing off the walls.

The man holding Kallie let go of her, backing away, continuing until he came up against the wall. The other security guards pulled back to join the first. A gasp escaped the receptionist.

The scientists gaped, frozen in spot. Even Adam seemed too shocked to move. The only one not locked in place was Kallie.

She rushed across the room. "Jerreon." His name came out as a whisper this time.

"My One," Jerreon said aloud, reaching for her.

Kallie slid her arms around him, aware of the bandage and other visible cuts. Tears ran down her cheeks as she pressed her face to his chest, placing a kiss over his heart. "My One." She stretched up to kiss him.

His lips caught hers. He kissed her fiercely then leaned back to frame her face with his hands, gazing down at her in reverent awe. "You found me." He brushed his thumb over her cheek and dipped his head to touch his lips to hers again, savoring her.

When the kiss ended, he leaned against her. Kallie took his weight, feeling the slight trembling in his body.

"Let us leave this place." He looked past her, daring the scientist or the guards to object. Those in the room remained silent.

Kallie held him tight to help support him as they crossed the room. Adam fell in step with them.

"Wait." The head scientist squeaked out, regaining his nerve as they reached the door. "Please."

Jerreon stopped, halting Kallie. Together they all glanced back.

It was Jerreon who answered. "You did try to keep me alive. I will consider talking to you in the future, but you never should have kept my wife from me." With that, he touched his lips to her cheek, and they walked out.

Edward had the car door opened before they reached it. Kallie went in first, reaching out for Jerreon as Edward and Adam helped ease him in. He sighed, collapsing back into the seat, totally spent. His eyes closed. Panic gripped Kallie. Jerreon's hand found hers and he intertwined their fingers.

"Do not fear, My One. I just require rest." His words were measured with pain.

"I have your medical kit. What do I do?" Kallie asked.

He cracked his eyelids, shifting his head to look at her. "You have it here?"

"Yes." She pulled it from her purse.

He released her and reached for it, but she got it open first. He removed a large patch. "Place this over the wound. It will help with the healing."

"What about the pain?"

"The red container. Remove one of the thin strips and place it under my tongue. It will control the pain for a full day. In the yellow container is another slip to go under my tongue also. It will stimulate the healing process and regeneration."

"I can give you both at the same time?"

"One right after the other. They dissolve rapidly." He closed his eyes again.

Kallie gave him the one for pain first. He didn't look at her, just parted his lips and lifted his tongue. It was already gone before she got the second strip out of its container and to his mouth.

The wrap on his ribs presented a dilemma until Edward handed back a multipurpose tool that had a pair of scissors. Kallie made quick work of getting rid of the bandage, though she was aware of the seriousness of his injury.

She tried to be calm, but a cry still escaped her. A dark bruise covered his side. Almost in the center of it was a gash. Even tended it looked frightening to her, though the weakness in him was more so. It was something she didn't associate with him.

His hand rose to brush her cheek. "Have no fear. I will be well now that I have you with me." He closed his eyes and slept.

CR&O

Eighteen hours later, Kallie came awake to the reassuring sound of Jerreon's steady heartbeat in her ear and the feel of him pressed securely to her. He still slept peacefully. In the faint glow of the morning light, she could see his breathing stronger and more regular, and his coloring appeared better.

She'd been so worried when he had collapsed in the limo's back seat. He hadn't even stirred when Sam, Josh and Edward carried him inside and up to bed. Twice he'd awakened just long enough to eat and drink a little before sliding back into a deep sleep.

Kallie reached for him in her mind as she stroked her hand lightly over his heart, making sure not to get anywhere near the bruise on his ribs. It had been so close.

Warmth flowed through her and one of Jerreon's large hands settled over hers, pressing it to his chest. There was a slight shift and his lips brushed her temple.

His chest rose and lowered with a deep sigh. "My One." The endearment sounded slightly hoarse and gravelly, but never better.

Kallie rose up enough to look at him.

Jerreon smiled and touched her cheek. "Have no fear. I am well."

"Are you, really?" She searched his face for the answer.

"I am. It may take a couple days to regain all my strength, but the healing is well on the way to complete. Remember, I can never lie to you."

"I was so afraid I'd lost you." The fear she'd been holding onto slipped out to be brushed away by the gentle touch of his fingers.

"I came a long way to find you. With my duty done, I am free to make my life, and it looks greater than I had ever hoped."

"Government men came here again last night. I met with them briefly. They requested that you contact them in the future. I told them that it would be your choice, if they gave us some space," she added.

"I will meet with them." His lips twitched. "After we have had some space. This is my world now, too. I have much to learn before I make many ripples in it." He ran his fingers over her chin, tracing the sensitive skin of her neck. "You found me."

"The dolphins helped," she whispered as she got lost in his aqua eyes.

"Most interesting creatures." His gaze drifted over her, lingering when they touched her lips. "We shall have to go visit them later. I would like to swim with them." His mouth lowered slowly. "For now, I would like to celebrate the life I never thought I would have."

Their lips met, forging a new place, made only of their love.

Epilogue

Jerreon gripped the ladder, pulling himself smoothly out of the water, sending a final mental farewell to the pod of dolphins that he'd been swimming with. It had become a weekly event to take the boat out to swim and interact with them. He enjoyed the bond they shared.

His gaze settled on the figure sleeping on one of the couches. His pleasure soared. Sun kissed Kallie's skin making her glow. She was so beautiful, so gloriously perfect. His bond with her also became stronger every day. She was the most precious thing to him.

He would marvel forever at how his life turned out. He'd truly thought in going after Lysias, he was giving up his life. Instead, he'd found it. He'd found love and a home here. A place he fit, maybe even better than his own world.

To his relief, the government had backed off after he agreed to do some development work for them. They had even agreed to let him pick his projects. They had assigned him a handler he found pleasant to work with, and Adam stepped out of retirement to be his manager. It made life convenient since they'd moved into his house, giving Adam the family he longed for.

Family. Kallie shifted as if feeling his gaze on her. Her hand went to the slight swell of her abdomen. Unable to curb his desire, Jerreon reached out with his mind and picked up the flutters of life growing there. He hadn't told Kallie yet there were two of them, twins, a boy and a girl.

The doctor said that on the next visit she would take a picture of the baby. Kallie would find out then, but until that time, he decided to keep the knowledge to himself since Kallie was already worried about so many things.

He picked up a towel and dried his shoulders and chest, rubbing it over his hair before draping it around his neck. His gaze locked on eyes the color of the sky. Kallie's lips curved up as joy filled her face.

"Sorry, I didn't mean to fall asleep." She stretched.

"It's all right." He settled beside her. "You need your rest." His hand moved lightly over the gentle mound."

"I probably should have swum longer."

"It was long enough. You do not want to over-tax yourself."

"Not much chance of that with everyone watching over me."

He leaned down and kissed her nose. "I enjoy watching you. It gives me pleasure." He stretched out next to her, kissing her again. "You give me pleasure." He let the truth of his words flow from him as he eased her into his arms.

"My love. My One."

About the Author

I grew up in a small town in Wyoming loving the outdoors, sports, art, and reading Hardy Boys books. After reading them all at least a half dozen times, I started writing my own stories.

For thirty-three years I was married to a wonderful, honorable man. I'm mother of five children and grandmother of nine, eight boys and one girl, with hopefully more to come. I love traveling. Through my husband's work and vacations, I have visited much of the United States, all over Europe, Canada, Mexico, China, Thailand, Cambodia and Australia, giving me many intriguing locations and experiences for my stories.

I am a storyteller. I write the classic hero story because I think there's a need for more heroes, love, and adventure in our lives. I'm not out to change the world with my writing; I'm just hoping to make your day a little better.

Hope you enjoy.
Alysia S. Knight

Please feel free to visit me through my website:

www.alysiasknight.com

www.ingramcontent.com/pod-product-compliance
Lightning Source LLC
Chambersburg PA
CBHW032119170626
46808CB00006B/2017